Matthew Hale, Edward Stephens, Berman Le Roy Edgar

A Collection of Modern Relations of Matter of Fact

concerning witches & witchcraft upon the persons of people - To which is

prefixed a meditation concerning the mercy of God, in preserving us from

the malice and power of evil angels

Matthew Hale, Edward Stephens, Berman Le Roy Edgar

A Collection of Modern Relations of Matter of Fact
concerning witches & witchcraft upon the persons of people - To which is prefixed a
meditation concerning the mercy of God, in preserving us from the malice and
power of evil angels

ISBN/EAN: 9783337382704

Printed in Europe, USA, Canada, Australia, Japan

Cover: Foto ©Andreas Hilbeck / pixelio.de

More available books at **www.hansebooks.com**

A

COLLECTION

Of Modern Relations of

Matter of Fact,

CONCERNING

𝕼𝖚𝖎𝖙𝖈𝖍𝖊𝖘 & 𝕼𝖚𝖎𝖙𝖈𝖍𝖈𝖗𝖆𝖋𝖙

Upon the Perfons of People.

TO

Which is prefixed a Meditation concerning the Mercy of God, in preferving us from the Malice and Power of Evil Angels.

Written by the Late

Lord Chief Juftice Hale,

UPON

Occafion of a Tryal of feveral Witches before him.

PART I.

LONDON.
Printed for *John Harris*, at the *Harrow* in the *Poultrey*.
MDCXCIII.

Price, 1s.

Licensed,

18. May, 1693.

Edward Cooke.

ADVERTISEMENT.

Mathematical Divinity : Or, A plain Demonstration from the Holy Scriptures, that the Times of this World, were Fore-appointed by the Covenant made with *Abraham* : And determined to be according to the Measure of the Age and Fulness of Christ. Kept Secret since the World began, but is now made plain upon Twelve Tables, in a Solar Calendar, as familiar to the Understanding as a Common Almanack. With a full Proof, that this is the last Generation, which shall not pass away till all things be Fulfilled, and the Gates of Righteousness be Opened. Being the Result of many Years Study. By *Elias Palmer*.

Printed for *John Harris*, at the *Harrow* in the *Poultrey*. 1693. Price, 1 s.

THE
PREFACE.

IT was not to convince the Atheists and Sadduces of this Age, of the Existence of Spirits, and by consequence of a Deity, that I began this Collection. They have the Works of the Creation, both of the Great and of the Lesser World, and an admirable Scene of Providence exhibited to the rest of Man-kind in the Posterity of Abraham, and Recorded in the Sacred Writings, which, if they were disposed with well defecated Minds (gently putting by the Leaves and the Prickles, and the mean outside Covering, whereby they are Veiled from the Prophane) to inspect the internal Form and Composure, and deeply Contemplate the admirable Accomodations of all the Parts, the Design and Tendency of the Whole, and the Secret Powers by which all is Sustained and Ordered, they might (by the help of a certain Divine Light, which doth often illustrate such Souls so employed) discern a more Noble Evidence and satisfactory Conviction of those things, which the Ignis Fatuus of a vitiated Natural Understanding (however improved, as is imagined, by the accomplishments

of

of what we commonly call Learning, but is in truth but a superficial thing, in respect of true Knowledge) cannot receive; *and be assured, that* Christianity *is indeed a Noble and Divine Philosophy, cast out like a Ball, among the Children of Men, that they should catch it that catch could; and accordingly is very differently, and by most very unworthily entertained in the World; not only by the sensual Swine, and by the Muckworms, but by such as would be thought to be of a more generous Strain, Cocks of the Game, and yet prefer a Corn of Barly and a Feather, before an inesti-mable solid Jewel. But not only their Wills, which are a great Byas upon the Judgment, but the Minds and Consciences of most of these People are so Corrupt-ed, that they cannot, or will not acquiesce in these Matters, even in greater Evidence than what they free-ly act upon in Matters more agreeable to their own Genius and corrupt Affections, being as averse to sub-ject their Understanding to the Divine Wisdom, as their Wills to the Laws and Will of God, tho the Subjection of the one is no less necessary to the attainment of the great end of Man, accordingly designed in the Divine Methods of Providence, than that of the other. And therefore to have undertaken such a Work as this for the Service of such People, I can hardly think would have been to much purpose ; and besides, it would have obli-ged me to such Proofs and Evidence for the satisfaction of others, as I conceive not so absolutely necessary for my*
                                                                purpose

The Preface.

*purpose in many particulars ; though I shall lay no
farther stress upon any of the Relations, when I come
to make use of them, than I am satisfied they may
reasonably bear.* But my Design *is this :*

Being well satisfied that much of the Good and
Evil, *which occurs* in the World, *not only in relation
to particular Persons, but whole Families, Cities, and
Nations, which is commonly attributed to Humane
Management, or I know not what blind Fortune or
Chance , is in truth* produced *by the Secret prevalent
Energy and Operations of certain Invisible, Intelligent
Agents, which not only order and dispose divers Occur-
rences, which to us Mortals seem very minute and in-
considerable, to be Occasions of great Consequences, but
do also insensibly, and yet effectually bind and impede, or
excite and promote, the Actions of Men, to produce Events
some much short, some beyond, and some contrary, to their
Designs : And that* our common Notion of Spirits,
*that is, of those Invisible Agents, which I conceive to be of
very different Natures and Powers, are greatly and
unhappily mistaken : And lastly, that much of the
Evils, which afflict Mankind, are effected by Spirits of ·
an inferior Nature and Power, and but of the next
degree in knowledge and Power above us Mortals, and
such as are usually imployed by Witches and Magi-
tians : I suppose that a better Understanding of the
Nature, Power, and Operations of these Spirits, of the
Means by which they get Advantage against us, and*

of

The Preface.

of the Means whereby we may either prevent the same, or be relieved and extricated out of their Power, would be a matter of no little Use and Benefit to Men. And in order to this I have begun **A** Collection *of Mo-*dern Relations of Matters of Fact *concerning Spi-*rits, *but principally of* Apparitions *and* Witches; *intending in Conclusion to put together my Obser-vations upon them, and what others I have met with in print of this or former Ages, for this purpose.*

And because this Wicked, and, even in Things wherein they think themselves Wise, Foolish Age, have strangely imposed upon themselves, or been im-posed upon by the Efficacy of the Devil or his Instru-ments, to a Disbelief *of the being of Witches, or of much of that Power, which they exercise through the Instruction and Assistance of those Spirits, and by con-sequence of their Agency in many Mischiefs and Evils, which we ignorantly attribute to other Causes: And also of some Means, which might be useful to detect them, and to disappoint their Wicked Operations; whereby many innocent and good People are left ex-posed to their Malice, who might otherwise be re-lieved; I thought fit to begin with a Publication of part of my* Collection *concerning* Witches, *reser-ving divers others which I have for a more Compleat Information, and my Collection of Relations of Appa-ritions till another time: And in the mean time shall be very glad of any good Information or Assistance in*

any

The Preface.

any thing relating thereunto; Wherein I defire only Certainty as to Matter of Fact; and then how Incredible foever it may feem to the Vulgar, or fuch as are skilled in the common Notions of Philofophy. I care not: For I am well fatisfied that divers great Truths cannot but feem fo to them.

To this I thought it very proper to prefix a Meditation, though not finifhed, of that no lefs Wife, Profound, Sagacious and Ingenuous, than Juft and Good Man, the late Lord Chief Juftice HALE, concerning the Mercy of God in preferving us from the Malice and Power of Evil Angels; which he wrote at Cambridge the next Lord's day after the Tryal of certain Witches before him at St. Edmund's-bury, whom he there Condemned, and ordered to be Executed, after a long Tryal from Seven or Eight in the Morning till Seven or Eight at Night, wherein he called to his affiftancs divers Phyfitians, and other learned Men; and at laft after a full and careful Examination, the Jury finding them Guilty, he paffed Sentence upon them with full Satisfaction of the Juftice of their Verdict. There is a Relation of it in print, written by his Marfhal, which I fuppofe (is very true, though to the beft of my Memory, not fo compleat, as to fome obfervable Circumftances, as what he related to me at his return from that Circuit. But that he was well fatisfied in it may be perceived by his Writing this Meditation fo immediately upon it. And
there-

The Preface.

therefore I think it very proper for this place, not only for the ufe which well-difpofed People may make of it, but also as an Evidence of the Judgment, of fo Great, fo Learned, fo Profound and Sagacious, fo Cautious, Circumfpect and Tender a Man in matters of Juftice, and efpecially in matters of Life and Death, upon fo great Deliberation, (for he knew by his Kalendar before-hand what a Caufe he was to Try, and he well knew the Notions and Sentiments of the Age) and upon fo folemn an Occafion ; to check and correct the Impiety, the Vanity, the Self-conceitednefs, or Bafenefs of fuch Witch-Advocates, as either confidently maintain that there are no Witches at all, making their fhallow Conceptions an adequate meafure for the extent of the Powers of Nature, and of the Wifdom and Power of God; or contrary to their Duty and their Oaths, make light of the Examination and Tryal of them, when brought before them. Such Perfons may have caufe to be afhamed of themfelves, after notice of fuch a Judgment, and others may hereby be admonifhed what to think of them, if they perfift in fuch Affertions, or Pretences.

A

A
DISCOURSE
CONCERNING

The great Mercy of God, in preferving us from the Power and Malice of *Evil Angels.*

Written by Sir Matt. Hale *at* Cambridge 26 Mar. 1661. *Upon occafion of a Tryal of certain Witches before him the Week before at* St. Edmund's-Bury.

1. **T**HAT *there are—fuch evil Angels,* it is without all queftion: The *Old Teftament* affures us of it, as it eafily appears upon the confideration of the Temptation of our firft Parents; the Hiftory of *Abimeleck* and the Men of *Shechem*; the Hiftory of *Saul* and the Witch of *Endor*; the Hiftory of *Micaiah* and the falfe Prophets; the Hiftory of *Job*; the Prophecy of the Defolation of *Babylon,* wherein *Jim* and *Zjim* and the *Satyrs* were Prophefied to Inhabit: The *New Teftament* more explicitly and abundantly clears it, by the Hiftory of the Temptation of our Lord ; the *Demoniacks* of feveral Symptoms Cured by our Lord and his Apoftles; the Proceffion of

the

the Evil Spirit, and his return with feven other Spirits; the
Vifion of the Fall of *Satan* from Heaven like Lightning by
our Saviour; the feveral affertings of it in the Gofpel and
Apoftolical Epiftles; the Prince of the power of the Air;
the Spirit ruling in the Children of Difobedience; the Kingdom of Satan; Principalities and Powers in high Places, and
more frequently yet in the *Apocalyps*: It is alfo confirmed to
us by daily *Experience* of the Power and Energy of thefe
Evil Spirits in *Witches,* and by them.

2. That thefe evil Spirits have likewife a great meafure of
Power, and a greater meafure of *Malice,* appears in the fame
Scriptures and by Experience. The greateft Strength and E-
nergy of any corporeal Creature, is in the vigourand power
of thofe Natural and Animal Spirits that are within them
The great fwiftnefs and ftrength of the Lyon, the Wolf, the
Tyger, and of the ftrongeft of Men, is the exerting of thefe
Vital and Animal Spirits, without which their Bodies, tho
of the exacteft Model and Compages for ftrength, were but
a Trunk and *iners moles.* Certainly therefore thofe Sepa-
rate Spirits that are not clogged nor encumbred with Mattter,
have a greater ftrength and energy, which is evident in thofe
Poffeffed *Demoniacks* both in the Gofpel and in known Experience, who could not be holden by the ftrength of Men,
when Poffeffed with this powerful and malignant Influence.

3. And yet *their Malice* to the Children of Men is more
extenfive than their Power: It began with the Firft Man in
Innocence, and it hath improved ever fince. The evidence
both of his Power and Malice, is moftlively feen in that difplay
of the Invifible Adminiftration and Exercife of it towards *Job*;
that it contented not it felf with any Bounds; his Goods,
his Children, his Name, his Body, the very Peace of his Soul
and Mind were not enough to content or quench it; info-
much, that had there not been a guard upon his Life his
Malice had alfo feized that: And which is yet more, his
Malice againft the everlafting Soul of Man is unfatiable, as
appears in that exprefs defcription of the Tempting of our
Lord,

Lord, Tempting him to Prefumption ; to Defpair ; to Apo-
ftacy from God : And this he did not only out of a particular
or perfonal Malice againft him; but as in his firft Temptation
of the Firft *Adam,* his Malice was not only at him, but at
the whole Kind, which in a great meafure he effected: fo
in his Tempting of our Lord, he aimed not only Perfonally at
him, but in him at the *totum genus Humanum* : For tho poffibly he might be ignorant of the hypoftatical Union of the
Divine Nature to our Lord; yet doubtlefs he did fufpect that
much of the good of Mankind was depofited in that Trea-
fury, which if he could have fhattered and broken, he had
exquifitely fatisfied the extent of his Malice againft Mankind.

4. This *Malice and Power* of that Evil one is much *advan-
taged* in reference to Man. 1. By his great *Experience and Subtilty.* 2. By his *Invifibility and Swiftnefs,* whereby he can
fecretly and powerfully infinuate and mingle himfelf with
the Subject he means to mifchief : He knows the Avenues
into Man ; and he knows how moft fubtily and unfufpect-
edly to feize upon them : In reference to *the Body of Man,* he
knows his Humours, his Temper, his Diftemper, and hath
the advantage of the higher Ground, as *Perfeus* had in his
fight with the Monfter in the Fable; as the Eagle in his
fight with the Dragon : He can watch his Advantage and Un-
difcovered can derive into him a malignant Air, or a poyfonous Fume, or a venomous Infufion ; His Experience in Natural Caufes; his Ability to difcover fit Actives, and to ap-
ply them effectually to Paffives ; his acquaintance with the
Natural Conftitutions, and his opportunities to difturb, or
invenom it ; his Speed and imperceptible Motion in infinu-
tion of himfelf, and his Experiments upon the Body renders
it, upon a bare natural account, much fubject to his Power.

5. And no lefs advantage hath he upon the Soul, Firft in
refpect of it felf and its own fpiritual Nature, whereby in all
probability he can fecretly and immediately infinuate himfelf
with it, and Perfwade, and Excite, and Deceive, and Abufe,
as a fubtil Man can deal with another of more fimplicity :

* 2   For

For it feems altogether as reafonable upon a bare natural account, that one Spirit may communicate with another in a Kind proper to their Nature, as one Man may communicate to another, in a Kind fuitable with his Nature. 2. And principally *in refpect of the manner of the operation of the Soul of Man in Communion with the Body*, whereby fhe hath a kind of dependance upon the Body's Conftitution, and by a difturbance or diforder in that, become fubject to a diforder in her Actings: Upon this account he can difturb the Blood into Cholar, or Luft; abufe the Fancy with falfe reprefentations or difturbances in Truth; corrupt the Organ of the Senfe, or the Species which they receive; inrage, and difcompofe the Humours of the Body, mingle Ingrediants with them, that fhall impede or corrupt the actings of the Soul. And as thus he can corrupt within, fo he can by *obfervation of the prevalence* of any Luft or Paffion, and of the juft *and true feafon*, when it is at the height, fit it with a Temptation that fhall draw it out to Action. When *Achan*'s covetous humour is high, he can unvail the Wedge of Gold and the Babylonifh Garment. When *David*'s Security and Idlenefs, and poffibly high and delicate Fare, hath raifed up the Luft of his Flefh, he can prefent him with a *Bathfheba*. Thus partly by *his own* Wifdom, Experience, malicious Vigilancy, Invifibility, Strength and Power; partly by our *own* Weaknefs and Infirmity, partly by *the Correfpondence* he hath with our Tempers and Difpofitions, he is able to make advantage upon us, either by internal Corrupting, or by external Alluring or Inciting us to what is hurtful and prejudicial.

6. Since therefore it is apparent that he wants neither Power, nor Opportunity, nor Malice, to mifchief us, it remains, that certainly *the obftruction of the executing of that Power doth not arife from himfelf*; for his Malice is unfatiable; it is his bufinefs every day to go about feeking whom he may Devour: And unqueftionably his Malice would carry him to the execution of the utmoft of his Power, either to deftroy Mankind, or at leaft to make them Slaves to his Kingdom.

dom. *Alexander* who was most certainly the most Ambitious Prince in the World, could not be near so fond of bringing the World under his Subjection, as this Prince of Darkness is. Those that he cannot make his Vassals, he would soon extirpate and exterminate out of the Bounds of his affected Empire: And on the other side, the obstruction is *not from our selves*; we are too weak to deal with him; he was too hard for *Adam* in his Innocence, and therefore must needs be too hard for us in our corrupted Estate. And if it be said, there was but one to one, we are many to one, or at least to few; we deceive our selves herein, for *they are Numerous*: One Man was possessed with a Legion, in the Gospel: But if it were otherwise, yet the Agility and nimbleness of those impure Spirits is great, and their dispatches speedy; they are *Itinerarii & Circumferanei*, walking to and fro through the World.

7. It remains therefore, that the power and malice of this great Enemy is checked and controlled, and *limited by a higher Power*; it is *Regnum sub graviori Regno*: And he that hath shut up the Sea in Bars and Doors, and said, *Hitherto shalt thou come, and no further, and here shall thy proud Waves stay,* hath likewise limited and confined this proud, and malicious, and powerful Adversary within his Sphear and Limit, and chained up this unruly and ravenous Woolf, so that he cannot go one Link beyond his prefixed Bounds.

8. These *Bounds or limits of the Power and Activity of this Adversary* are many: we may reduce them into these four, *viz.* 1. The Law of their Subjection. 2. Providential Dispensation. 3. Ministerial Resistance. 4. Natural Impediments.

I. The first restraint is *the Law of their Subjection*: for tho those impure Spirits are like Rebels and Malefactors against their Lord, and have an habitual Opposition against him, yet they are under his Dominion; tho they hate to Obey him, they dare not disobey him; tho they have not the love of the Law of their Being, yet they are under the Cohersion and fear of that Law. Just as there be among Men many vile

People

People that yet dare not act their Villany for fear of Punish-
ment; and if they do, they do it by stealth and secretly : So
doubtless those Evil Angels are under a fear of Offending,
and do smart for it. Government is the Ordinance of God,
as well in the Invisible as the Visible World : And this seems
plain to me by that Petition of the evil Spirits to our Saviour,
that they might not be sent to the place of Torment, even
before their last and final Judgment. There are certain
Torments for their Extravagancies, inflicted by an Invisible
Oeconomy, which they fear and dread as much as Malefactors do the Whip and the Pillory. And upon this account
partly it was, that *Satan*, tho he had naturally power to
have afflicted *Job*, durst not attempt it without leave and
permission from God.

II. *Providential Dispensation* : And this is the same over
Men and Devils : It naturally lies in the Power of one. Man
to Kill or Hurt another ; yet that same Superintendency of
Divine Providence, without which a Sparrow falls not the
Ground, prevents one Man from doing all the mischief to another that naturally lies in his Power ; and the same preven-
tion and Providential interposition, hinders the activity of
the Evil One from doing all that Mischief he naturally can
among the Children Men. And this was that Hedge and
Fence that God had made about *Job*, and all he had ; and
till that were removed, the attempts of *Satan* were vain and
idle to have broken in upon him.

III. *Ministerial Impediments*, and these are of two kinds.

1. Such Impediments as concern the Soul only, and the im-
mediate Agency there. *Satan* he disturbs, and provokes, and
perswades and tempts to Evil, but the *Divinæ Graciæ Admini-
cula* counter-perswade. The Son of God came into the World
to destroy the Works of the Devil, and there is a perpetual
contest between these two, for the Principality and Dominion over the Children of Men ; on the one side, the Devil
and his Angels they Fight by their Method, and Temptati-
ons, and Allurements, and Insinuations, to win over the
Children of Men to the Kingdom of Darkness : On the other
side

fide *Michael* and his Angels, the Angels of the Covenant, and the fecret and powerful Agencies of his Grace and affiftance, take all opportunities to reduce Men to the Obedience of God, to their Duty to him, confirms them in it, detects and difcovers, and convinceth the Tempter, and upholds the Spirits of Men againft him : He will convince the World of Judgment by judging the Prince of this World, that is, by detecting his Sophiftry, his Falfity, and the ill confequences thereof.

2. Such as concern the inward Man and the outward Man alfo, the Miniftration of the *Good Angels,* who are as diligent to counter-work the Evil Angels in their Mifchiefs, as they can be fedulous to inflict them ; they are Miniftring Spirits. When the Devil was ufing a flight to gain the Body of *Mofes* to make an Idol of him, *Michael* refifted him. The Evil Angels are full of Power and full of Malice againft the Children of Men ; and on the other fide, the good Angels are no whit inferior to them in Power, and are Benevolent and Loving to the Children of Men, and do many and many times when we know it not, prevent us from many mifchiefs that thefe malevolent Regiments of Hell would inflict upon our Bodies and our Souls. And doubtlefs, as we fee in the vifible Adminiftration of the World, or of any one Kingdom thereof, there is continual Diligence on one fide by feditious turbulent minded Men to break the Peace of a Kingdom or City, or place, which is with much diligence, watchfulnefs, and vigilancy, attended and prevented by wife and good Men ; fo there is no lefs care and vigilancy, and counterworking by the Pure and Good Angels, againft the mifchievous defigns of thefe evil Spirits againft the Children of Men.

IV. *Natural Impediments* to the working of that Evil Spirit.

1. *In reference to the Soul* and inward Man. God hath fortified the Will of Man with the priviledge of Liberty ; tho thofe Evil Angels may follicit, perfwade and tempt, yet Almighty God hath placed this Bar in his way, *viz.* The

freedom

Freedom of the Will, that all the Devils in Hell cannot take from him: It is an impregnable Fort, that can only be taken by Dedition, but never by Storm or Assault. And this is partly the reason of that Text, *Resist the Devil and he will flie from you*. He knows that where there is Resistance of the Will, there is no entrance for him, and gives over the Assault.

2. In reference *to the Body* or outward Man. He cannot ordinarily exercise any Violence upon the outward Man, but by the Mediation of things Corporeal, and most ordinarily by the mediation of Mankind: He cannot kill a Man but by the Sword of a Man-slayer; nor rob or plunder, but by a *Caldean* or *Sabean*; nor infect the Body, but by the means of a Witch. And all this God hath most wisely ordered in this manner, that tho the Impure Spirit it self be out of the reach or regiment of Human Justice or Government; yet the Instrument, without which he cannot ordinarily work, is within the reach of Human Justice and Government: whereby the wise and good God hath consequently as it were, reduced him, *viz.* in his Instruments, without which he cannot act, under the very Power of Human Laws and Government. I say, ordinarily he cannot act any external mischief upon Man, but by such Means and Instruments as are under the cohersion of Human Laws. I say, *Ordinarily*, for when this *Iræ Divinæ satelles* is Commissioned from the God of Heaven, he may act immediately from himself, according to the tenor or extent of his Commission; but Ordinarily and Naturally he cannot.

Not Finished.

Doctor Pordage *his Relation of the wonderful Apparitions, Visions, and unusual things which were seen in his Family, in the Year,* 1649.

DOctor *John Pordage* Rector of *Bradfield* in the County of *Berks*, being the Eighteenth of *September* 1654, Charged with certain Articles then and afterward exhibited to the Commissioners for ejecting of Scandalous Ministers; amongst other things, for entertaining at his House one *Everard* a reputed Conjurer; and that he had frequent and familiar Converse with Angels; and concerning the Vision of a Dragon, and Apparitions of Spirits, *&c.* As to the Entertainment of *Everard*, he answered and confessed, that about four Years before, he was received into his House for about three Weeks and no longer, but not as a Conjurer, but as a workman at Harvest; and that he never heard the least intimation that he was ever suspected to be a Conjurer, till after his Departure, but afterward was strongly enclined to believe that he was: And concerning the Vision of a Dragon, and Apparition of Spirits, *I will not confess,* saith he, *any Apparition in particular,* till they be proved, left I should seem to accuse my self, they being brought in as a Crime against me, and as Instruments to Condemn me: Yet, in general I acknowledge, that some four Years since, there were many strange and wonderful Apparitions in my House: But, what can these in Justice amount to, tho attested by Oath, and confessed particularly by my self, when brought before those who profess themselves Christians, and are acquainted with the History of the Holy Scriptures? Pray, was not *Job* a pious, sincere, and eminently Righteous Man? Yet, how was he scared with Dreams, and terrified with Visions, *Job* 7. 14. Did not *Zachariah* the Prophet, Chap. 3. see *Satan* standing at the right hand of *Josua* to resist him?

Did

Did not *John* *(Rev.* 12.*)* in a Vifion behold a great red Dragon that made War with *Michael* and the Holy Angels? And was not Chrift himfelf tempted of the Devil, by Voice and Vifion? *Matt.* 4. 6, 8. Now, *the Servant is not greater than his Lord,* Jo. 15. 20. and therefore not exempted from the like attempts of the Devil. I befeech you confider, whether this Earth be not the Place where the Devil walks up and down feeking whom he may Devour? How then can *Bradfield,* or any other Place, be exempted from his Appearing when God permits? And may not all this be for the manifefting of his Glory, Goodnefs and Power? And who can tell whofe Family may be next expofed by God's permiffion, to be tryed and proved by the Reprefentation of *Satan?* And I defire you ferioufly to confider how any fuch Apparitions raifed by the Devil, and permitted by God for his own Glory, argue me either Ignorant, Scandalous, or Infufficient : Surely it rather argues that he hath bleft me with a ftrong Faith, in that he permitted fuch great Tryals, and made me inftrumental to overcome them by Prayer and Fafting. If it can be proved I ever fo much as looked toward the unlawful Art of *Black Magick,* or that any Evil Spirits were raifed up by any compact of mine, explicit,or implicit ; or that thofe Evil Apparitions were fubdued and overcome by any other means than by God's Bleffing upon our Fafting and Prayer, I fhall judge my felf worthy of Punifhment. But otherwife, it is hard meafure to be Profecuted for the Malice of the Devil toward me, inflicting what I was Paffive in, and could not help, efpecially by thofe who profefs the Chriftian Religion, and know that the God of Heaven ruleth over all, permitting and difpofing whatever comes to pafs.

This is the fum of what I meet with in his anfwer to the Commiffioners concerning this part of his Charge : But in an Apology afterward, he inferted a particular Relation concerning the Vifions and Apparitions therein alledged againft him, as here followeth in his own words.

I

I Do judge that God doth call me forth to make a free and open Difcovery of thofe *Wonderful Apparitions*, *Vifions and unufual things*, which fomewhat above four Years fince *were feen* and permitted by the Lord to be *in my Family*. And if all that read this, can but receive and judge of it by that Rule and Principle from which I write it, they will be fo far from judging me, as that they cannot but blefs God for his Favour and Mercy to me; and the more admire his wonderful Works and the greatnefs of his Power.

What I intend here to declare, I fhall difpatch in thefe *three Particulars*. 1. In relating what I have acknowledged to many Perfons I have Difcourfed with. 2. Many confiderable things, which I have never Difcourfed but to fome Friends. 3. The good effect of this upon my felf and others of my Family.

1. I confefs, That in *Auguft* 1649. there appeared in my Bedchamber about the middle of the Night, *a Spirit in the fhape of* Everard, with his wearing Apparel, Band, Cuffs, Hat, *&c.* Who after the fudden drawing of the Bed-Curtain, feemed to walk once through the Chamber very eafily, and fo Difappeared.

That very Night there was another Appearance of one in the form of *a Gyant*, with a great Sword in his Hand without a Scabbard, which he feemed to flourifh againft me, having the figurative fimilitude of a green Tree lying by him.

After this had continued for the fpace of half an Hour, it Vanifhed; and there fucceeded a third Appearance, which was very Terrible, being in the fhape of *a great Dragon*, which feemed to take up moft part of a large Room, appearing with great Teeth and open Jaws, whence he often ejected Fire againft me, which came with fuch a Magical Influence, that it almoft ftruck the Breath out of my Body, making me fall to the Ground.

Now, you muft know, that thefe three were dreadful Apparitions, and very terrible to the fenfitive Nature, and

B 2   might

might have caufed a great Diftemper in it, had I not been
fupported in an extraordinary way by the Miniftration of
the Holy Angels againft the evil effects of thofe extraordinary unufual Apparitions, the laft of which continued till
the day began to dawn, and then Difappeared.

2. In the Second place I fhall proceed to declare thofe
extraordinary things which few have been yet acquainted
with, which yet were then feen and experimented amongft
us.   I fay then there were *two Invifible, Internal Principles
opened and difcovered* to us, which may be called *Mundi Idæ-
ales,* being two Spiritual Worlds, extending and penetrating
throughout this whole vifible Creation, in which many particular things were difcerned fuitable to the Nature of thofe
Worlds.   Now, thofe two Principles or Worlds, feemed
very much different one from another, as having contrary
Qualities and Operations, by which *they work upon this vifible
Creation,* which we fee diftinguifhed and differenced into
variety of Creatures, fome Poyfonful and Noxious, others
Wholfom and Harmlefs, accordin gto the difference and
contrariety of things in the Internal World, upon which the
External doth in fome meafure depend, as ftanding in them,
or rather proceeding from them.   Now, thefe could not have
been feen, had not that *inward Spiritual Eye,* which hath
been locked up and fhut by the Fall, been opened in an extraordinary way in us.   Befides, we had our *other Internal
Spiritual Faculties* of Spiritual fenfation opened to difcern
their *various Objects* within thofe Worlds: Which Objects
by reafon of their Qualities, may be differenced into Good
and Evil.

But I fhall here firft prefent the Objects of that Internal
World, which may be called *Mundus Tenebrofus,* or the Dark
World.   Which Objects by our correfpondent inward Fa-
culties or Senfes were then difcerned and made known to us.

Firft then, as to the Objects of the internal *Sight,* when
this Principle or World was Opened, we beheld innumerable multitudes of Evil Spirits, or Angels, prefenting themfelves in appearing Diftinctions of Order and Dignity, as
Powers,

Powers, Principalities, Dignities. My my meaning is, there
feemed to be Inferiority and Superiority ; Governors and
Governed ; *the Princes* of this dark World and their Subjects,
which prefented themfelves as paffing before our Eyes *in
State and Pomp*, all the mighty ones appearing to be drawn
in dark Airy Clouds, Chariots with fix, or at leaft four
Beafts to every one; befides, every figured fimilitude of a
Coach, was attended with many *inferior Spirits*, as Ser-
vants to the Princes. But concerning *the Shapes and Figures*
of the Spirits, you muft know they were very Monftrous, Terrible, and Affrighting unto the outward Man. Thofe that
drew the cloudy Coaches appearing in the fhapes of Lions,
Dragons, Elephants, Tygers, Bears, and fuch like Terrible Beafts. Befides, the Princes and thofe that attended
them, tho all in the fhapes of Men, yet reprefented themfelves monftroufly mifhapen, as with Ears like thofe of Cats,
cloven Feet, ugly Legs and Bodies, Eyes fiery, fharp and
piercing. Now, befides thefe Appearances within, the Spirits made fome wonderful *Impreffions upon vifible Bodies without*, as Figures of Men and Beafts upon the Glafs Windows
and the Cealings of the Houfe, fome of which yet remain.
But what was moft remarkable was the whole vifible World
reprefented by the Spirits upon the Bricks of a Chimney, in
the form of two half Globes, as in the Maps. After which,
upon other Bricks of the fame Chimney, was Figured a
Coach and four Horfes, with Perfons in it, and a Footman
attending, all feeming to be in Motion, with many other
fuch Images, which were wonderful exactly done. Now,
fearing left there might be any Danger in thefe Images,
through unknown Conjuration and falfe Magick, we endeavoured to wafh them out with wet Cloaths, but could
not, finding them Ingraven in the fubftance of the Bricks,
which indeed might have contiued till this day, had not
our fear and fufpicion of Witch-craft, and fome evil defign
of the Devil againft us in it, caufed us to deface and oblite-
terate them with Hammers. Now, what the Devil's End in
the former Apparitions, and thofe figurative Reprefentations
was,

was, the Lord knows: But it was certainly Evil; Even as it was was againſt Chriſt, when he ſhewed him (in Viſion) the Kingdoms and Glory of the World, to make him fall down and Worſhip him. But God's end in permitting it was very good, even to bring us nearer to himſelf, in a ſtronger dependance upon his Eternal Power, and to make us more watchful againſt the Subtilty and Power of *Satan*, as you will ſee afterwards, when I come to ſpeak of the Effects of thoſe things in reference to our Selves. But to ſhut up this Relation of the Objects we ſaw in this Dark World, I muſt add this, that were but the Eyes of Men opened to ſee *the Kingdom of the Dragon* in this World, with the multitudes of Evil Angels, which are every where tempting and enſnaring Men, they would be amuſed, and not dare to be by themſelves without good Conſciences, and a great aſſurance of the love and favour of God, in protecting them by the Miniſtration of the holy Angels.

2. As to the Objects of the outward *Smell*, I muſt let you know, that within the three Weeks ſpace in which theſe Wonders appeared, at ſeveral times the Evil Spirits and Angels did raiſe up ſuch noyſom poyſonous Smells, that both the inward and outward part of thoſe that were exerciſed with them, became much diſturbed and offended: For through the ſympathy betwixt the Body and the Soul, the ſulphurous helliſh Smells much exerciſed both by Magical Tincturation.

3. In reference to the Objects of *Taſt*, You muſt know, that ſometimes both in the day and night, we were exerciſed with the loathſom helliſh taſts of Sulphur, Brimſtone, Soot and Salt mingled together. Which were ſo loathſom to our Natures, as that they were ready to cauſe great Diſtempers and Nauſeouſneſs in our Bodies; but the Inviſible Power of *Jehovah* ſupported us beyond our own Strength.

4. In relation to our inward and outward *Touch*, we were much exerciſed both in Body and Soul. As to our Souls, we ſometimes felt ſuch ſtrange Magical Wounds and Prickings by the fiery Darts of the Devil, that none can expreſs,

but

but thofe that have been exercifed in fome meafure, as *Job*
was, who felt the Poyfon of thofe invenomed Arrows, which
came upon him by the permiffion of the Almighty; which
like the Scorpions in the *Revelations*, fting and pierce thofe
they touch.   As to our Bodies, we found material Impreffions from the Powers of Darknefs, very noxious in themfelves to our natural Spirits and Life, but cheerfully born
by Invifible fupport, and quiet fubmiffion unto the Will of
God.

But to conclude : By thefe wonderful and ftrange Exercifes, we could not but have ftrong apprehenfions and lively
refemblances of the Torments and Miferies of Hell, where
Sulphur, Fire, Brimftone, poyfonous Smells, Darknefs, monftrous horrid Shapes and Sights are the entertainment of the
imprifoned Spirits.

But, now I come to the other Internal World, which we
may term *Mundus Luminofus*, or the Light World, which
with its various Objects was then likewife opened to the inward Senfes.

Firft then I fhall here fet forth the Objects of the inward
Eye, which were then feen by us.   There appeared then
to our inward Sight, multitudes, almoft innumerable, of
pure Angelical Spirits, in figurative Bodies, which were clear
as the Morning-Star, and tranfparent as Chriftal.   Thefe
were *Mahanaim*, or the Lord's Hoft, appearing all in manly
Forms, fending forth a Tincture like the fwift Rays of the
hot Beams of the Sun, which we powerfully felt to the re-
frefhing of our Souls, and enlivening of our Bodies.

Now, beholding the multiplicity, variety and beauty
of thefe Spirits, with the various Objects and Wonders of
this World, Cloathed in the pureft Tincture of Light and
Colour, we could not but blefs the God of Heaven, who by
the Eyes of Wifdom and Hand of Power, brought forth fuch
Glorious Creatures, and now fhewed them in their feveral
Beauties to us in a time of Tryal and Temptation.

Secondly,

Secondly. In relation to our inward sense of *Hearing*, there were many *musical Sounds and Voices*, like those which *John* heard upon Mount *Zion*, then heard by us; the sweetness, harmony and pleasantness of which cannot be expressed, nor that Spiritual Joy and Delight which by them was infused into our Souls, uttered by the Tongue, being ready to ravish our Spirits into the highest Praises of the Eternal *Jehovah*.

Thirdly. In relation to the Faculty of *Smelling*, the Tongue can hardly express those *Odours* of Paradise and heavenly *Perfumes* which then were smelt, piercing into the very Spirit with a cherishing Tincture; besides that quickning Virtue, which by them was communicated and insinuated into the Spirits of our outward Bodies, which like a Cordial, had been able to have renewed the strength of our languishing Nature.

Fourthly. Our Sense or Faculty of *Tasting* was very pleasantly entertained with those invisible Dews, which were sweeter than Hony, or the Hony-comb, and therefore deserve to be called the Dews of Heaven; with which instead of Food, we were many times wonderfully Refreshed.

Fifthly. In relation to the Sense of *spiritual Contaction,* that was also delighted with its heavenly Objects: For none can utter that pleasing Impression, which the burning Tincture of this Light World afforded us, coming like a hot Cordial into the centre of our Spirit, being sensibly felt in the inward Parts, so as to cause much joy and heavenly Pleasure, which penetrated through our Souls, giving us occasion to bless, praise and magnifie the Lord.

Thus for the space of three Weeks or a Month were we exercised inwardly and outwardly, through that great Conflict which was betwixt those two Worlds and their Inhabitants: The Dark World sometimes afflicting us with dreadful Shapes, abominable Smells, loathsom Tasts, with other Operations of the Evil Angels: The Light World at other times opening and relieving us with odoriferous Perfumes, most sweet Dews, glorious Visions, and Angelical Harmony, which the Lord favoured us with, to shew his

extraor-

extraordinary Love in thus Succouring us in extraordinary Exercises and Tryals.

Thus much for those two internal Worlds, spread throughout the visible World; in which the Evil and good Angels are more immediately than in this visible Air, to which they cannot be commensurate by reason of their spiritual Natures, each of them abiding in their distinct Principle, the the one sort being in Joy, the other being in Torment, the one in Light, the other in Darkness, according to the Scripture.

Besides these two Worlds, we had an opening of the *Eternal World,* called in Scripture the World to come, (or κειμένην τὴν μέλλουσαν, *Heb.* 2. 5.) from the futurity of its full and clear manifestation, and a precursory entrance into the most Holy Place, by a Divine Transportation into the Glory of the Majesty, agreeable to that of St. *John,* 17. 24. *Father, I will that they also whom thou hast given me, be with me where I am, that they may behold my Glory which thou hast given me, &c.* Here were seen, heard and felt unutterable Mysteries of that Kingdom, which are not yet to be divulged, in regard of the Pride, Ignorance, Prejudice and Envy of many in the World, being reserved for those humble gracious Spirits, which are waiting in Silence for the second coming of the Son of Man.

But, now it is time to come to the *third Particular,* which was *the effects and Impressions* left upon our Spirits by these wonderful Exercises and Manifestations.

After this, we began more clearly to see that *Strait and Narrow Way* which leads to Life Eternal, which we call *the Virgin Life,* or the Life of Purity and Righteousness in its Perfection, being the Life of fixed Love: In any thing short of which, the perfection of Virgin Life cannot consist. So that meerly to abstain from the concupiscible lustings of *Venus* under the Spirit of this great World, is but the Life of outward Chastity, and but a particular Branch of the other. 'For the 'Virgin Life is not attained till the Will of the Soul is 'brought through Death to be so Passive, as to will, desire

C

'and

' and act nothing but what the essential Essence of Love
' wills, moves and acts through it : For till then the Soul
' cannot be a pure Virgin, nor live without all Desire and
' Imagination ; which must all cease before the pure Life of
' God can come to be all in all.

This Life of Virginity was placed fore-right as to the inward Eye of the Mind, being that mark of Persecution, at
which we are to aim in our pressing toward the Resurrection of the Dead. To this Wisdom, that Eternal Virgin (*Prov.*
8. 20, 23.) as a Leading-*Star* invited us, calling to follow
her in the way of Circumcision, Resignation and the Cross,
in the way of total *Self*-denial, and forsaking of all for her
sake, in the way of Annihilation and conformity to Christ's
Death, by which we saw undoubtedly we should come to
Christ's Resurrection, Ascention, Glorification, and Fixation
in the love of the Holy Ghost, the third and last Dispensation.

Here we clearly saw the danger of looking back to the
External World, and of putting out our Imagination into
the Inward World, or the Kingdom of the Dragon ; or
of resting in the openings and delights of the Inward Light
World. For by turning back into the delights of the Sen-
ses, we saw the Soul would become Bastial ; by turning to
the left Hand and imagining into the Kingdom of the Dragon,
in awakening the fire of Wrath and Subtilty, devilishly and
dangerously Wicked ; by turning to the right Hand in imagining into, and taking too much complacency in the Visions, Illuminations, Tinctures and Enthusiasms of the Light
World, we saw the Soul might become elevated into self-
conceit, and tinctured with Pride, and be in danger of neg-
lecting the Death of the Cross, which is the only safe Path
into eternal Rest and Fixation.

Here then we were shewed, that the way which leads
up to the Virgin Essence the New *Jerusalem,* was strait and
narrow, as upon the Breadth of an Hair, so that we were to
turn no way either on the right or left Hands, but
stand without Lusts, with our Eyes fixed upon the Being of
Love,

Love, preffing forwards after Fixation in the Eternal Houfe of God, there to become immoveable Pillars, no more to go out, but there always to bear the Name of God, and the Name of the City of God, which is *New Jerufalem*.

And now for the fpace of this four Years, ever fince the time of thefe great Manifeftations, we, by the Grace of God, have enjoyed the exercifes of our Spiritual Senfes, which never fince have been fhut, neither ever will be, except through voluntary Tranfgreffion and Difobedience, we Apoftatize and run back into the Earthly Nature, or turn afide to center in fomething fhort of the pure Life of Virginity, which calls us from the External, through the Internal, into the Eternal World; which is that Kindom prepared for us from the beginning of the World.

But Thirdly, after this extraordinary time of Grace and Mercy to us, we enjoyed not only a clear leading convicting Light upon our Underftandings, but likewife received from the Lord a ftamp and ftrong impreffion of Power, moving our Wills to follow this Light through the Death of all things, to come up into the perfect Life and Image of God, that fo we might be transformed into that Righteous Nature, which we fo clearly behold through Divine Light. Hence we came to live in a greater abftraction from our Senfitive Nature, in a conftant watchful practice of the Crofs, in reference to all external and internal Objects, which might by entertaining our Affections, hinder our progrefs to God. Hence alfo we came to live a more devoted, ftrict, dedicated Life, fequeftring our felves from the World and worldly things, giving our felves almoft continually to Prayer, Fafting and waiting upon God, in dying daily to all felf-Ownments, Relations and Proprieties, in which moft are intangled, to the great prejudice of their Spirits. And in this way we have ever fince continued, endeavouring to be wholly conformable to the Death of Chrift; in renouncing our own Lives and proper Wills, as oppofite to the Life and Will of God, experimenting thofe profound Myfteries of the Crofs of Chrift, which are hidden to moft in the World. But what Joy,

C 2

Life,

Life, Power, divine Pleasure, and Heavenly Communion, the Lord hath blessed us with in this our dying resigning Progress, I shall wrap up in Silence, together with those blessed Secrets of the Kingdom, which in these few last Years past we have been acquainted with, to the comfort of our Spirits in this sad time, when we are judged and condemned of the World, in the participations of Christ's Sufferings.

The

The Discovery of Thirty and Two young Girls in the Cloister of Madam *Bourignon* at *Lisle*, found to be Witches. Related by her self and the Continuator of her Life.

Anthoinette Bourignon *was Born at* Lisle *in* Flanders 13 January, 1616. *Her first appearance in the World was not without some Deformity, her Forehead being grown all over with black Hairs, her upper Lip drawn up to her Nose, and her Mouth gaping wide open*: But *the hairs of her Fore-head afterward fell off of themselves, and her Lip was restored to its proper Posture by the help of a Chirurgeon, and she grew more and more Comely; yet her Mother had never any great Affection to her; but loved her least of all her Children; but her Father loved her best of all, possibly the better for being of his own Complexion, he being an* Italian, *whereas all the rest who were Fair, possibly took after their Mother, who was of the Country of* Lisle. *She was it seems from her Child-hood to be conformable to her Saviour in Sufferings: And her first Persecutions were by her own Kindred and nearest Relations, even her Mother and her Sister, which had this happy effect upon her, that she became very Retired and Serious in her tender Age. And she then received such strong impressions and attractions by the Grace of God, as soon as she had the use of Reason, that her Thoughts and Discourses were such as seemed not to come from a Child, but from one of well grown in Years. She always thought she should be in some other Place, and enquiring where was the Country where Christians Inhabit, expressed a desire to go thither. And when she was told she was then in a Country of Christians, she could not believe it, because* Jesus Christ *was born in a Stable, and lived in Poverty; but the People there had stately Houses, rich Furniture and plenty of Mony, &c. But such Discourse would not down there, but was turn'd into Ridicule, so that she was constrained to keep silence and say no more of it. When she grew up, she would not Marry, but had a mind to enter into Religion, or become a Nun*

among

among the Carmelites, *where she hoped to find such true Christi-*
ans as she desired ; but therein soon found her self mistaken ; and
thereupon betook her self to a Solitary and Retired Life, with
great Austerities, exercising various acts of Charity as she saw
occasion.

After the Decease of her Father in April 1648, *her Mother,*
Brother, *and all her Sisters being Dead before, having recover-*
ed what belong'd to her from her Mother-in-Law, she at first
intended to have gotten together a Society of Religious Virgins :
But one day as she was walking there met her a Stranger, whom
she did not remember to have ever seen before, and told her, that
what she purposed, she could not effect, nor would it be to any good
purpose, for there were Nunneries enough ; but there were great store
of poor Children every where, who wanted good Education ; and
there could be no better Work thought on, than to take some of
them, and Educate them from their Childhood in Religion and
Virtue, and such Employments as might enable them to get a
comfortable livelyhood. This Man went by the name of Jean de
St. Saulieu, *and proved at last a very Wicked* Man : *But in the*
mean time prevailed with her to undertake this Work ; and the
rather because one Jean Stappart *a Merchant, had already de-*
signed a House at Lisle, *with near* 50 l. *per an. for that very*
purpose, and had already taken in about a Dozen poor Girls. With
him she contracted in the Year, 1653, *and had their Agreement set-*
tled by Publick Notaries : And in November *that Year, she made*
her Entrance into the House, and soon had the number of her Girls
encreased to about 50. *She kept them at first only as in an Hos-*
pital or School ; but finding some inconveniencies in that way, she
thought fit to be recluse ; and in November 1658, *by permission*
of the Bishop, turn'd it into a Cloyster, where she kept her Girls
under strict Discipline, and to very good Orders, both as to their
Work and as to matters of Religion : But after she had passed about
Seven years in these pious Exercises, three Years after she was
Cloystered up, no less than Two *and thirty of these young Girls*
were discovered to be Witches. Of which, and of divers remark-
able Particulars thereunto appertaining, the three following Rela-
tions furnish us with a considerable History.

The

The Firſt Relation, *Tranſlated out of her Tract, Enti-tuled,* La Parole de Dieu.

113. AFter my being Encloiſtered, I had more leiſure and convenience to attend daily the Inſtruction of the Children. I diſcovered more of their Wickedneſs, and preſſed them the more to good Living : But I perceived their Souls but little the better, unleſs Exteriorly. They were more Modeſt and Obedient, keeping to the Rules of Prayers Enjoyned them. People that ſaw and heard them Pray and Sing, thought them little Angels : But I was always of the mind that they were without the Grace of God; but yet I know not by what means. Some of them came of themſelves to Confeſſion every Week, tho it was cuſtomary but once a Month. They willingly heard good Lectures, Faſted the whole *Lent*, though they were not obliged to it. Made their Humiliations every *Friday*, by telling their Faults in the Hall. Underwent without regret all the Penances which were enjoyned them. There was nothing of ill obſerved in their Comportment, but that ſome of them would not work willingly. Others were enclinable to Lying and to Thieving, for which they were Corrected, and many times with profit and amendment. I put all thoſe out of the Houſe who were not content with a Chriſtian Life. The reſt declared themſelves to be more contented than they were before. I would no more take ſo great a Number again, well perceiving that there would be leſs Confuſion in it. I Prayed to God to know of him whether he received Glory by it. He anſwered me, theſe are but *Humane Accomodations*.

114. This I have very much experienced ſince, ſeeing that neither the Children nor their Parents ſought more than their Temporal Advantage; as poor People for the moſt part.

are.

are little follicitous for the Glory of God, or the Salvation of their Souls, fo that their Bodies are at Eafe. This often troubled me : But afterwards confidering that their Souls were Cultivated as well as their Bodies, I went on in my upright Intention, to gain them to God. My Confeffor very much approved of this Exercife; but often asked me whether I would not accomplifh my firft Defigns. I anfwered, Yes, but that God muft fhew me the Way and the Place appointed, and that his time was not yet come. Many Perfons grew to have a kindnefs for the Houfe, and added divers foundations to it. We had the Mafs every day; a great concourfe of People came to us. Upon St. *Anthony*'s day we had a Plenary Indulgence, and the three Paftors celebrated High Mafs, and other Divine Services with us.

115. One day as I came into the School where all the Children were at Work, I faw a great number of *little black Children with Wings* fly about their Heads. I told them my Vifion, exhorting them to beware of the Devil, who moft certainly environed them.

116. After I had paffed about Seven Years in thefe pious Exercifes, it happened one day that as *one of thefe Girls* was to have been Corrected for fome fault, we *fhut her up into a place call'd the Prifon.* About an Hour after fhe was there, fhe came out tho no Body opened her the Door. And as all the other faw her come into the School, they changed their Countenance and looked Pale. Returning, I faw it was fhe who had been Lock'd up. She asked me Forgivenefs, promifing me to Amend. I asked her who it was who opened her the Door? She faid a Man. I told her fhe was Mad; becaufe no Man came into the Cloifter, and bid her take her Work. She who had fhut her up, was then Abroad : And when fhe returned and faw this Girl at Work, fhe was amazed, and faid, Who has opened the Door for her ? I carried the Key with me. I made her go to the Place where fhe had fhut her up, where fhe found the two Doors Lock'd as fhe left them when fhe went out. I took the Child a part into my Chamber to Examin her. She faid that a Man who was her

Friend

Friend, came and opened the Door for her, and she call'd him always in her need. I was afraid that this must be the Devil. I sent the Pastors word that they should come and hear the Matter, who having strictly examined her, told me, that there was great appearance that she was a Witch. I would not believe them. Nevertheless I immediately turn'd *her out of the House,* fearing that some Evil Spirit had brought her thither, and that she might trouble the House. She was between Thirteen and Fourteen years of Age. I now called to mind, that the whole Fury of Hell was to be armed against me: Wherefore I pray'd that strength might be given me to Oppose and conquer them.

117. About three Months after, it happen'd that another Girl was to be shut up, of about Fifteen Years Old. She said, that the Devil made her to commit the Thievery; and that he came to her by Night. I turn'd her out also, thinking to purge the House. But yet three Months after we discover'd *another* who was but Thirteen Years Old. She was to have been Whip'd: But saith she, Do not do it, and I'll tell you who it is that makes me do this Mischief. Taking her aside into my Chamber, she told me that it was the Devil. I asked her whether she knew the Devil or not? She said ay, he is almost always with me. I asked her what manner of Person he was? She said he was a handsom young Youth a little bigger than her self; that he had marked her upon her Head; and that she had given him her Soul, and had renounced God and her Baptism. I forbid her to tell this to any Body. However I sent for the Pastors being very much troubled to think what this should be, believing it an Illusion, or a Frenzy.

118. When the Pastors had Examin'd her, they said, that I ought not to put her away, for that there was a great Misfortune among these Children, which was to be search'd to the bottom; for that this Girl had declared to them, that there were *two more* among them such as her self. They Examined those two, who declared that they were so, and that there were *two more* besides. We Examined on further,

and

and found that all the said Girls were in Compact with the Devil: For they related such particulars which they could not know unless they were true, or else they must have very much studied these Matters. Now they were in Number *Thirty and two*, and no more, who had all contracted this Mischief before they came into the House, and had learn'd it some of their Relations, and some of their Companions, and all in different Places, different Towns, Villages and Parishes.

119. I was in great perplexity, having never believed that there was such Creatures in the World, at least very rarely; and that they had something peculiar outwardly to be observed about them; but that these Children performing all pious Exercises, I could not perswade my self that they were such. But be it as it would, I asked the Pastors if there was no Remedy. They said there was, since that they had been gained by the Devil before their age of Reason. I told them that we must spare nothing, but use all possible Endeavours. The Chaplain, Pastors, and the Capuchin Fathers, Exorcised them two Hours a day, each Man twice a Week. The Pastor of the Parish where the House stood, which was St. *Saviour*'s, came often to interrogate them to discover more and more the Truth, and to endeavour to reconcile them by Confessions and Penances.

120. He wrote down their Examinations for his Memory sake. They formerly declared that they had daily carnal Cohabitation with the Devil; that they went to the Sabbaths or Meetings, where they Eat, Drank, Danc'd, and committed other Whoredom and Sensualities. Every one had her Devil in form of a Man; and the Men had their Devils in the form of a Woman. And that there were so great a number of Persons at these Nocturnal Assemblies, where every Devil brought from day to day their Love whether Male or Female, that no Assemblies were ever seen so Numerous in the City as in those Sabbaths, where came People of all Qualities and Conditions, Young and Old, Rich and Poor, Noble and Ignoble, but especially all sorts of Monks and Nuns, Priests and Prelates; and that every one took his place as they do in the World: that they there Worshiped a Beast,

with

with which they committed infamous things, and then at laſt they burnt it; and every one took up ſome of the Aſhes, with the which they made Men or Beaſts to Languiſh, or Die; declaring ſome of them particularly, that they had made uſe of them to kill Poultry and other Creatures.

121. After they had declared all theſe things to the ſaid Paſtor and to me, they would ſometimes ſay, that there was nothing in it; then again they would ratifie all by confirming it anew: And after that would deny it; and then confeſs it again. So that I continued Eight Months in theſe Exorciſes, letting no Body know it but thoſe Divines. During this time between whiles they made General Confeſſions, wept in appearance of Sorrow and Repentance: But all was but Counterfeit, their Hearts being addicted to ſenſual Pleaſures, which the Devil gave them. They had not the leaſt deſign of changing, to quit theſe abominable Pleaſures, as one of them of Twenty two Years old one day told me. *No*, ſaid ſhe, *I will not be other than I am; I find too much content in my Condition; I am always Careſſed.* I have had of them from Eight Years of Age to Twenty two. The Elder of them told me, *We are often afraid of being with Child by the Devil; for we ſhould thereby be diſcovered that it was by the Devil, becauſe we never ſee any Men come into the Cloiſter.*

122. About this time a Woman of the Town was very importunate with me to take a Girl of Nine years Old out of Charity. I yielded to her Deſire. But thinking to teach her and make her Work, ſhe would do nothing; ſo that one day going to Correct her, ſhe ſaid, the Devil held her Hands, and ſhe could do nothing. The others Laughing cry'd, that ſhe was out of their Gang. And indeed after I had Examined her, ſhe told me more particulars than the others had done, ſaying that ſhe could kill Cows tho they were two Leagues diſtant. I immediately turn'd her off, having enough of that ſort already. The Woman who had recommended her to me, underſtanding by this Child what paſſed in the Houſe, and that every one had confeſſed this Secret, ſhe preſented a Petition againſt me to the Magiſtrate, ſaying

that

that I abused the Children, and that I should take away their Reputation by believing that they were Witches, and that she gave this Advertisement to the Magistrate, out of Charity and Love that she bore to those Children.

The Second Relation, Translated out of her Tract, Entituled, La Vie Exterieur. §. 23. 1661.

81. BUt the Fifth discovered it self about three Years after I had been Cloistered up, and began by a young Wench of the Village of about Fifteen years of Age, who having done some Offence, was to be corrected by being shut up by her self, which the House-keeper by my Order did. And after having shut up the said Girl, she took the Key with her, and went out of Doors: But about an Hour after she was gone, the Girl came into the School where the others were at Work, who seeing her coming, turned all Pale; and being asked what made them change their Countenance? They told me that they saw before them at the School door the Girl that had been shut up, whose Name was *Bellot*; and being bid to come in if she was at the Door, she came up and ask'd me Pardon for her Fault, promising to Amend. I asked her if she had not been shut up by the House-keeper? She said yes. How then came you forth, said I? She held her Tongue for some time; but being pressed to Answer, she said, that a Man had let her out. This I took for Raving, because I knew that no Man, or other Person, could be in the House. But not being willing to make further enquiry before the rest, I bid her take her Work and be good hereafter. In a little time after, when the House-keeper returned from her business Abroad, and saw this Girl at her Work, she was *Astonished*, crying, Who is it that hath opened the Door for this Child? I had shut three Doors upon her, and see here the Keys at my Girdle. I went out of the School to inform my self from
the

the House-keeper, if she had really locked up the Doors? she answered me, she had; and going to the Doors, found them all three Lock'd, as she had left them. This thing troubled me; and after Dinner I call'd the said Girl into my own Chamber, to know of her how she got out of so fast a Place. She said that a Man opened the Door for her. I asked what Man this might be, and if she knew him. Yes, she said she knew him very well, and that he was the Devil. At which I was struck with Horror, saying, The Devil's a Spirit, he is not a Man. Tho he be a Spirit said she, he comes to me in the shape of a Man; and as I call'd him to my Assistance when I was shut up, he came to me, opened the Door and let me out. I asked her how long she had known this Man-Devil (or Devil of a Man?) She said all the days of her Life: That her Mother had taken her with her when she was very Young, and had even carried her in her Arms to the Witches Sabbaths or Assemblies, which were held in the Night; and that being a little Wench, this Man-Devil was then a little Boy too, and grew up as she did, having been always her Love, and Caressed her Day and Night. I could not comprehend this Discourse, having never hear'd the like in my Life.

83. I immediately wrote to the three fore-mentioned Pastors, to desire them to come to my House, where there was a Girl who told me things which I had not capacity enough to understand; desiring that they would come and Examin her to know what it might be: They came all three together the same day, and having Examined the Girl, she declared to them that she had given her Soul to the Devil, and had renounced God; and to confirm the donation of her Soul, she had received a mark upon her Foot: That this Contract had been made at Twelve Years old; but that long before that time this Love of hers had accompanied her, and carried her at Nights to the Witches Meetings in great Castles, where they assembled to Eat, Drink, Dance, Sing, and act a thousand other insolencies, with many other particulars

ticulars which fhe could not know unlefs fhe had been a
Witch, or had ftudied Books of Magick, which could not
be, fhe beginning then but to learn her Letters, having been
but a little while in my Houfe. I told the Paftors that I
would not endure any longer fuch a Perfon in my Houfe,
left fhe fhould fpoil my other Girls ; and I placed her out
the fame day with a Woman whom I knew to be of a good
Life, from whence a little time after a Man came and took
her away, faying, he had Married her Mother, and he
would be her Father; and fo I never heard more of the faid
Bellot.

84. I was much troubled in my mind to fee that the Devil had yet fo much Power as to trouble a Houfe of Religion, of which I had undertaken the Government for the Glory of God, and the Salvation of Souls. I often Examined
my felf what fault I might have committed, that fhould give
the Devil fo much power as to fend a Witch into my Houfe,
when I thought there had been but few of them in the World.
And tho I could not believe that the faid *Bellot* was a Witch, yet
I found that the Devil had great Power over her. Not knowing however what fort of Creature a Witch muft be, having
often thought that Witches were ugly deformed Creatures,
or half Beafts, as they fay of them, that they do transform
themfelves into Cats, Horfes, and other Animals; fo that I
could not believe that this Girl was a Witch, tho the three
Paftors aforefaid, did affure me of it. I Pray'd to God to
difcover to me my fecret Sins, not knowing to what Caufe I
might attribute fo ftrange an Accident, which intruded it
felf amongft my good Intentions. However, I kept regular-
ly on the Difcipline of my Houfe, believing that I had got
rid of fuch kind of Perfons, by difmiffing the faid *Bellot*.

85. But three Months, *(viz.* after the Difcovery of a Second about Fifteen Years old, who is not here mentioned,
tho fhe be in the former Treatife, and was fent away three
Months after the firft; fo that this happen'd fix Months
after the firft. See *La. Parole de Dieu*, §. 116.—121.)

afterwards

afterwards we difcovered another, which faid and did the fame things. This was a Girl Born in the Town, which had always been Nurfed in the Village, of about Twelve Years old, who for the evil cuftom fhe had gotten of Stealing, was one day to have been Whipped; which being not willing to fubmit to, fhe faid fomebody had advifed her to Steal, whom fhe would tell me of if I would forgive her that time. I then forbore her, to the end I might know what evil Creature it was that gave her that advice. I call'd her into my Chamber alone, thinking I fhould difcover fome other of the Girls that Counfelled her to Steal; fhe prefently fell à Crying, and would not anfwer me a Word. But a little after fhe faid it was the Devil that gave her this evil Counfel. I gave a great Sigh, telling her that fhe faid this only to cover her Wickednefs, for that fhe could not know the Devil. She replied, that fhe knew him very well; that he was a Boy a little bigger than her felf; and that he was her Love, and lay with her every Night. I asked her how long fhe had known him. She faid, that being very Young and playing with the Girls in the Village, they ask'd her if fhe would go with them to the Dedication; that fhe fhould have good Chear and a Sweet-heart into the Bargain. And as foon as fhe confented, her faid Lover came upon a little Horfe, and took her by the Hand, asking her if fhe would be his Miftrefs, and fhe faying Ay, fhe was catched up into the Air with him and the other Girls, and they flew all together to a great Caftle, where they play'd upon Inftruments, Danc'd, Feafted and drank Wine: And that ever fince fhe had been there three or four times a Week; that at Ten Years old fhe had given her Soul to the Devil, renounced God and her Baptifm, and received a *Mark* from the Devil upon her Head; which we afterwards found to be true, for that fhe was infenfible in the place where the faid Mark was made; for we ftuck a Pin as long as ones little Finger into her Head, and fhe felt no Pain.

86. I

86. I immediately fent to the aforefaid three Paftors to come and Examin this fecond Girl, who faid almoft the fame things as the firft. And after that they had Examined her, they told me that fhe was alfo a Witch; and that I ought not to turn her out of my Houfe 'till I had difcovered whence this Misfortune came; that there muft be fome Witch in the Houfe that thus drew the Children after her. I followed their advice by keeping this Girl in the Houfe; but confining her in a Chamber feparate from the reft; where neceffaries were brought her and alfo her Work. One of thefe Paftors, call'd *Peter Salmon*, undertook to Examin her every day, to the end he might bring her to a good Converfion, to renounce the Devil, and to return to God: And asking if there were no more Children in the Houfe, who were fuch as her felf, fhe faid that there were two more that went with her every day to the Sabbaths. And having examined feparately the other two Girls whether there was any truth in it, they ingenuoufly confeffed, that they were bound to the Devil by a precife Contract, and had configned their Souls to him. Underftanding this, I refolved to fend away all the Children that I could, fearing that inftead of procuring the Salvation of their Souls by keeping them with me, they would by teaching one another their Wickednefs, all be Damned. I could not fend them away all, by reafon that the greateft part of them were fo poor, that they had neither Friends nor Houfes to be received in. And for this reafon I was ftill obliged to keep *two and Thirty*.

87. The faid Paftor *Salmon* began for his Memory fake to write down what thefe Girls had faid to him, being all three in diftinct Apartments: And having fpoken often with them, the two laft faid, that there were ftill two more in the Houfe, and that they for their pars need not be taken out from the reft. But asking them who the others were, they each of them named two different Names. And having Examined the faid Four, they confeffed that it was all true; and named each of them two different Names, which were of the fame Diabolical Company; fo that from Two to Four,

and

and from Four to Eight, we difcerned that the Thirty two yet remaining in the Houfe, were all in general, and each in particular given up to the Devil, by their own proper and deliberate confent: And that not one of them Contracted this Wickednefs in the Houfe, but brought it with them thither, having diverfly fallen into it, fome by their Fathers, fome by their Mothers, and fome by playing with other little Girls together, as they declared as well to me, as to the faid Paftor, who put all the Particulars which they told him in Writing.

88. I was mightily perplexed to find my felf confined to a Houfe with two and Thirty Creatures, who declared that they had all given their Souls to the Devil. The Maids I had for my affiftance went all away, leaving me alone with thefe wicked Wretches, with whom I was forced to Eat and Drink, at leaft what they Dreffed for me. I held divers Confults with the faid three Paftors, what was fit to be done upon fuch an Occafion. I propofed to difmifs them by degrees; but then I feared I fhould be guilty of the mifchief that they would do among Man-kind, when they were abroad; for they confeffed to me, that they had Killed both People and Cattle, which I alfo afterward found by Experience, they having killed all of a fudden thirty young Ducks, Cats, Chickens, and other Animals about the Houfe in lefs than two Hours time, which they have often Confeffed. Wherefore I could not honeftly turn them out, left I fhould wrong my Neighbours by fending them fuch Perfons as thefe, without giving them Notice; and by advertifing of them, none would receive them.

89. Upon this, I was greatly Difpirited, and could not fee what was the Will of God in this point. The Paftors on the other hand faid, I ought to let them all continue with me, and that they hoped they might convert them to God, becaufe they were engaged to the Devil in their Child-hood before they had the ufe of their Reafon; offering me to do their utmoft, faying that they would come every day to Advife and *Exorcife* them, and Pray for their Converfion. And

E   having

And having asked them if it were poſſible that theſe Creatures could be converted to God after having deny'd him and given their Souls to the Devil; they anſwered me that they might; that God was Merciful; and that as wicked as Men could be, they might be Converted ſo long as they were in this World. Which is very true; but ſince that time I have had ſufficient Experience that Perſons thus contracted to the Devil do not turn, becauſe they have no real deſire to be Converted, tho they make a ſhew as if they had.

90. I reſolved then to keep the ſaid Children with me, exhorting them all I could to be converted to God : And the ſaid Paſtors came every day one or other of them to Admoniſh them and to Pray with them. Which we did very ſecretly for the ſpace of about eight Months: During which time, the Girls made great ſhew of Converſion, by Tears, repeated Confeſſions, Prayers and attention to the Admonitions which were made them.

91. Many of them ſeemed to melt into Tears, when I ſpoke to them of the Judgments of God, Eternal Life, the Joys of Paradiſe, and the Torments of Hell. But this laſted not long. And when I Examined ſome of the eldeſt and moſt ſenſible of them whether theſe Tears were Feigned, and Counterfeit, or elſe Sincere; they anſwered me, they proceeded from their Grief for having denied God, and abandon'd themſelves to the Devil. But that this laſted no longer than whilſt they were ſpoken to, and had their miſerable Eſtate before them : That the Devil came preſently to them, and asked them, how they could leave him, and all the Pleaſures they had taken together? And Careſſed them ſo much, that they immediately made a new Contract with him, forgetting all the good Purpoſes they had taken before.

92. I asked them, if the *Admonitions, Exorciſms and Prayers of the Paſtors*, did not take away the Power of the Devil, from holding them thus ſubjected to him ? They told me that *the Devil Laugh'd at theſe Performances*; and that after the manner of a Monky he mimick'd the ſame Ceremonies that the Paſtors

Paſtors did; when they Kneel'd down to Pray, the Devil kneel'd behind them, and with a Book in his Hand he babled out the ſame words; and when the ſaid Paſtors Preach'd, the Devil made behind them the ſame Geſtures, and ſprinkled about the Holy Water; and alſo Confeſs'd them as the Paſtors did, imitating them in every thing in Deriſion and Mockery.

93. I asked them, *How they could* Pray or *ſing ſo many good Prayers* all the day long, when they were thus in League with the Devil? They told me, that he himſelf Pray'd and Sung along with them, by reaſon that their Prayers were without *Attention*: And that inſtead of ſinging to praiſe God, their *Intentions* were to ſing the praiſes of the Devil, wherein he gloried and valued himſelf.

94. I asked them how they could approach the Table of the Lord and receive the *Sacrament*? They ſaid, that the Devil invited them to do it as often as they could; and that the greateſt Penance that I could enjoin them, was to make them abſtain from this Sacrament, which was a Cloak for their Wickedneſs, and made them paſs for good Folk before the World. Beſides, that the *Devil wrought his greateſt Villanies with this Conſecrated Bread.*

95. I asked them, *How it was that they could* Faſt, even tho they were not obliged to it? For from Fourteen or Fifteen years old they would Faſt out the whole *Lent*. And when I would have hindred them, they Wept bitterly. They told me that they faſted but out of hypocriſie and to pleaſe me: And becauſe they had every night a Glaſs of ſtrong Beer, and a greater portion at Dinner than thoſe who did not Faſt. That for theſe Reaſons they did deſire to keep *Faſt*.

96. I told them that all theſe falſities would certainly bring them to Hell. Their anſwer was, that they very well knew it; and that they were aſſured to be Damned; but that the Devil promiſed them the ſame carnal and ſenſual Pleaſures in Hell, that they took with him in this World

97. I asked them if they were certain that this was the Devil, who thus entertained them; and if whethether they knew that there was a Hell and a Heaven before they came to live in my House? They told me, Yes, becaufe the Devil had taught them it, and had often Catechifed them, and taught 'em that there is a God, a Heaven and Hell, and a Devil; and that he that did the *Devil's* Will, could never fee God, but fhould be his Companion in Hell to Eternity. I was very much aftonifhed to hear thefe Difcourfes, having never thought that the Devil could teach fo good things, or excite People to Pray, Faft, and frequent the Sacraments, or to think of Heaven and Hell. Neverthelefs, by long Experience I have found it to be very true.

98. I asked them, how it was poffible that they fhould belong to the Devil from their tender Infancy, even before they had ufe of their Reafon? They faid, that that came from their Parents ; and when their Fathers or their Mothers are themfelves abandoned to the Devil, of neceffity all their Children are fo alfo till they arrive to the ufe of their Reafon ; becaufe that their Fathers and their Mothers have power over the *Souls* of their Children, until they come to ufe their own Judgment, and that then the Child receives its Free Will, and can make ufe of it to do Good or Evil : But that it was very rare when they had been *Sacrificed* and offered to the Devil by Father or Mother, even before they were Born, that they fhould withdraw themfelves from him, when they came of Years ; becaufe that the habit of Wickednefs is become Natural to 'em; and the Devil having entertain'd them from their Birth with Careffes and fenfual Pleafures, fo gains their Affections, that they will not quit them for any confideration, after having been allured to Senfualities, fuch as no Man could give them : For the Devil feigns to make them eat all forts of delicious Meat to their Tafte, all forts of pleafant Wines to their Pallate, all forts of Mufick, or Inftruments to their Ear; all forts of Beauty to their Eyes, and all Perfumes to their Smell, and all manner of Titillations to their Flefh: So that being brought up therein,

in, it is as it were impoſſible to have a mind to leave him. And therefore it is that they ſay, *We will not change our condition for the greateſt Pleaſure that Mankind can give us.*

99. I condoled with them their Misfortune, ſhewing them that this was all Deceit and meer Illuſion; that the Devil had no thing, nor could he give any thing. And to ſhew that they had neither eaten nor drank at the Sabbaths, they needed but obſerve their own Appetites on Mornings, when they eat great pieces of Bread and Butter, and would eat dry Bread if it was given them, which if they had eaten ſuch dainty Meat, they would not touch, nor could they eat ſuch groſs Meat ſo ſoon with ſo good an Appetite; for had they been at a Feaſt with Men and drank Wine as they ſaid they did at the Devil's Banquets, they would be Sick all the next day. They told me this was all true, but however they had the taſte and pleaſure of all theſe things, and therefore would not forſake 'em.

100. I informed my ſelf ſometimes as exactly as I could, to know how it was poſſible that a Father or a Mother could offer their Children to the Devil, inſtead of offering them to God who Created them, asking them in what manner this was Practiſed? They told me, that Perſons who were thus engaged to the Devil by a preciſe Contract, will allow no other God but him, and therefore offer him whatſoever is deareſt to them; nay, are conſtrained to offer him their Children, or elſe the Devil would Beat them, and contrive that they ſhould never arrive to the State of Marriage, and ſo ſhould have no Children, by reaſon that the Devil hath power by his Adherents, to hinder both the one and the other; and that this is effected in this manner.

111. When a child thus offered to the Devil by its Parents, comes to the uſe of Reaſon, the Devil then demands its Soul, and makes it deny God and renounce Baptiſm, and all relating to the Faith, promiſing Homage and Fealty to the Devil in manner of a Marriage, and inſtead of a Ring, the Devil gives them a Mark with an Iron Mark upon ſome part of the Body; which Marks they renew as often

ten as thofe Perfons have any defire to quit him. The Devil reproves them then more feverely and obligeth them to new Promifes, making them alfo new Marks for affurance or pledge, that thofe Perfons fhould continue faithful to him, and fo foon as they come to be able to beget Children, the Devil makes them offer the deifire which they have of Marrying, to his Honor : And with this all the Fruit that may proceed from their Marriage. This they promife voluntarily, to the end that they may accomplifh their Defigns : For otherwife the Devil threatens to hinder them by all manner of means, that they fhall not Marry, nor have Children.

The Third Relation, *Tranflated out of the* Continuaation *of her Life.*

La Vie Continuee. *Chap.* XV.

How Madam *de B. Difcerned by Supernatural things and by the Proper Confeffion of the Girls fhe Governed, that they were all in voluntary League with the Devil, and that they endeavoured to Murder her,* &c.

Firft of all, fhe was convinced, that the Children which fhe brought up in her Houfe, were of the number of thofe unhappy Creatures, by many Supernatural and Diabolical Aĉtions which fhe faw by them. For, they got out of Places when they were fhut up, without Keys : Then were things found in the Houfe which could not be brought thither but by means of the Devil ; fuch as little Balls of Poyfon, and a certain fort of Paper they were lap'd up in, which fome of them faid, were given to others of them at their Sabbaths, and which they affured her they had in their Chambers. There were found in their Beds fuch Filth and
Naftinefs

Naſtineſs as comes from Cows, which they confeſſed at laſt was communicated to them by the Devil, when he came to ſatiate their Diabolical Leachery. They killed living Creatures about the Houſe, as Fiſh, Cats, Chickens, and once Thirty little Ducks at one time, by a diabolical Powder, which one of them ſtrewed in the place where they were to paſs. And when Madam *de B.* asked her how the Devil could have power over thoſe little Creatures? She anſwered, Becauſe you pleaſed your ſelf yeſterday in looking on them: Which Madam *B.* acknowledged to be true, obſerving with ſome admiration how thoſe little Creatures Swam and provided for themſelves ſo well, being but juſt out of the Shell. She thereby experienced this terrible truth, *That the Devil hath power over whatſoever a* Man *placeth his affections in, when they are not upon* God. And indeed Man being Created only to take pleaſure in God, who ought to be his Delight; 'tis impoſſible but that a Curſe ſhould follow whatever breaks this Order.

2. Another time they made it Rain ſo furiouſly into the Common Room where they were at work, that Madam *B.* was forced to go out all wet as ſhe was. One of them another day having caſt ſome Powder into the Oven of the Houſe when they were Baking of Bread, tho the Oven was ſo hot that the very Bricks of it were red, yet the Bread which was put in remained there ſix whole Hours, no more Baked than when it was put in : And Madam *B.* having asked the Cook-maid the reaſon of it, ſhe ſaid that ſuch a Girl who had ſtop'd the Oven, had thrown in ſome Powder, and that the Fire would never touch the Bread, although it ſhould remain there all the day long; but that ſhe would take care when they Baked next, that that Wench ſhould not come near the Oven ; which being done, the Bread was Baked as throughly in two Hours time as Sea Bisket. Another time one of them thought fit to caſt a Charm in amongſt the Meat boyling in the Pot ; Where having boyl'd ſix Hours together, it came out as raw and bloody as it came from the Shambles. They have often ſaid ſince,
that

that were it not that the Devil was afraid that we fhould be convinced by extraordinary things, he would make us work Miracles; but he fears nothing like that. They declared that they had often given their Powders to the Mother Regent, which operated according to the intention of her who gave them. One day Madam *B.* finding her felf ill with a fore Throat, one of the Girls told her, *I know well enough what's the matter*; *it is but the effeEt of a little Powder, fhe'll be Cur'd in four days time, but not with the Ointments which are prepared for her.* All the Month of *January* and part of *February* in the year 1662, it was almoft every day difcovered, that fome one or other of thefe Girls had been corrupted in their particular Affemblies, befides their general Sabbaths, where they had Balls of Poyfon given them to Kill Madam *Bourignon*; and they would have Poyfoned the Paftor of St. *Saviours* Church, who was to come and Officiate and Dine there upon St. *Anthony's* day. As faft as thofe Poyfons were taken from them, which they ufually hid in their Beds, they got more, which St. *Saulieu* furnifhed them with in this Affembly, with defign never to have done till they had killed her. *We'll make fo many*, faid they, *that one of them fhall do at laft; and then when fhe's Dead, St.* Saulieu *fhall come here, with whom we fhall agree well enough, and then we may keep our Dancings in the School it felf.* Thefe Balls were put into the hands of the Governor and Secretary, when they came at laft to vifit the Hofpitals, upon the Complaint which Madam *B.* had made of the Matter: And the Secretary faid, when he took them away; *I carry off the Devil.*

3. 'Twould be impoffible to relate all that thefe Girls confefs'd when they were Difcovered, concerning themfelves, their Parents, their Education, their Companions, their Neighbours, and People of the fame Towns and Villages; nay, their very Paftors and their Lords, their Sabbaths and Affemblies, their Tranfports through the Air, where they faid they had been Tranfported over great Forefts in the Air, their Feet would fometimes touch the top Branches of

the

the Trees, as they flew to thefe Sabbaths, whofe devilifh
Ceremonies they did relate, their abominable Divertifements
and Whoredoms with the Devils in Human fhape, from
whom they faid they received fomething very Cold, of which
they were fometimes afraid to become with Child, and a
thoufand deteftable Devilries, which would be horrible to
relate; and which I will pafs over in filence, as alfo thofe
which are related by Madam B. her felf in the former Trea-
tifes, except fome few, which I had from her Mouth.

4. When this Mifchief began firft to appear, there was
one amongft them very Induftrious to difcover the reft,
which having done, and thereby thinking her felf to be
out of all fufpicion of being ftill of the Company, yet
at laft fhe was found out: But fhe conftantly deni'd it,
although the others did affirm that fhe went with them to the
Sabbaths; fhe defended her felf upon this Point, That there
could be no Colour that fhe who had affifted in the Difcovery of the reft, fhould be Guilty, and ftill an accomplice
of the fame Crime. Neverthelefs, this was the moft wicked,
falfe and cunning of them all. And this proceeding of hers,
was but an effect of her devilifh Cunning. This was fhe who
a little after faid, fhe would not renounce the Devil, nor
amend, nor did fhe defire to be other than what fhe was;
and was one of the firft of thofe upon whom thofe Diabolical Poyfons were found, with which they intended to Murder their Benefactrefs. She would have denied all at firft,
but at length confeffed, after which fhe denied it, and advifed the reft fo to do, and to make feigned Confeffions, advi-
fing them to deny all they had confeffed before. One day
as fhe was upon her Denials, when the Life of St. *Anthony*
was reading in their Prefence, wherein was mentioned a
Temptation that the Devil ufed by melodious Singing, Madam B. faying, I never obferved yet that the Devil Sung,
and I wonder at it; the Girl anfwered, O Mother, they Sing
fo delicately that you would be even Ravifhed to hear them,
How! do they Sing fo well faid fhe? Ay indeed, faid the Girl,
for they were Angels once. All the reft fell a Laughing: And

fhe

she was so confounded for having so openly confessed before
she was aware, that she knew not what to say; but endeavouring to excuse her self, one of her Companions said, Go,
Go, you have said too much that you have hear'd how
well they Sing; you cannot answer that. If I have heard
them, saith she with anger, you have heard them as well as
I. Sometime after she again confessed her self Guilty. One
of the reasons for which she said she would not be Converted then, nor renounce Satan, was that the Devil told them
sometimes that they might be saved well enough if they
were Converted hereafter; and that it would be time enough
if they repented upon their Death-beds, and were Converted then; and so they might take their Pleasures and Pa-
stimes, which the Devil gave them while they might have
them.

5. It happen'd about this time, that *the Devil* in a merry
Mood *Appeared to Madam B.* in this manner. There came
one and knock'd at the Gate of the Hospital, and asked to
speak with the Regent, who was then all alone without
assistance to help her in the affairs of so great a House. When
she came to the Gate, she there found *a little wrinkled wry-
mouth'd Woman*, yet very nimble and brisk, who offered her
her Service in her present occasion. Madam *B.* having never known nor seen this Old Woman, and seeing nothing in
her to recommend her, she told her she could not take her,
because her age and weakness were too great to undergo the
Labour and Orders of the House. But the Old Woman answered shaking her Breech, No, no, I have a great deal of
Vigor yet: I can Work, I can Watch, I can rise on Mornings, I can Fast, I can Pray, I can be a good Housewife,
you'll find I can do any thing; and began to Talk and Discourse very pleasantly, and with great earnestness to be taken in. But Madam *B.* being call'd away to speak with a
Physician who came into the Hospital, when she came back a-
gain to speak with the old Woman whom she had bid to stay,
found neither the old Woman, nor any appearance of her,
nor could she ever know from any Body who she was, or
whence

whence she came, nor had any Body seen her besides. She told the Doctor of it, who said, he saw her not as he came in. But the Girls fell all a Laughing, saying, it was the Devil, which they knew very well; and that he came only to play the Rogue with her. Of which she was afterwards satisfied.

6. Speaking to them one day of some Girls of the House that lately dyed with *great demonstrations of Piety,* they said, that they were also of their Number. And when she said, that that was impossible, because those Girls died in *Transports of Piety, and calling upon the name of Jesus Christ*; nay, that one of them said but the day before she Died, that *Jesus Christ had appeared* to her, and assured her that he would come fetch her to Morrow at such an Hour, when in effect she Died, singing and rejoicing that she was going to Paradise. These Girls fell a Laughing, and told her, that this Apparition of *Jesus Christ* was the Devil; that all those Prayers and Exclamations to God, were addressed to the Devil; and that by these words, God and Jesus Christ, by reservation to themselves they meant the Devil, to whom they directed all their Prayers; and that by the word Paradise, they understood no other thing than the Company of *Satan.*

7. Madam B. having asked one of them one day, why she did not confess this wickedness sooner: She answered, that being so common a thing, she did not think there was any harm in it, or a thing to be confessed, alledging to her that Millions of People of all degrees, were in the same condition, and that she scarce knew any others. She answered, Alas! you saw well, that I was no such Person. How say you then you scarce know ony others? O *Mother,* said the Girl, *you are not like other People, for there are very few such as you in the World.* They declared to her furthermore, that the Devils were almost always with them, whether they were in their particular Chambers, or in the common Room where they worked: But when Madam B. was there *they durst not appear:* That *they feared her so much,* that when

F 2
she

she but moved the Latch of the Door to come in, or when they heard her but walk, speak, or but cough, they immediately for fear vanished like Lightning : Which greatly confirms what Fr. *de la Croix* saith of *Souls strongly united to God*, that they *become terrible to the Devils*, as a Moth whose Wings are scorch'd at the flame of a Candle,is afraid to come at it again.

8. They confirmed often their Declarations in the presence of the three Pastors, who were Inspectors of the Hospital, who came to Examin them, and declared positively that they were Witches. Coming to Exorcise them for their Conversion, but in vain, one of them wrote down their Declarations, which were at last presented to the Magistrates, where they remained till such time as he should please to take cognizance of the Matter. It is true that the greatest part of them denied all again before the Court; but it was too gross an Imposture. They were threatned on the one hand and caressed on the other. Nevertheless, one of them notwithstanding all Menaces, remained firm in her first Declaration, that she was a Witch as well as the others; nor would she deny it tho she should have died on the spot. This poor Creature was engaged to the Devil from her Childhood, and when she came to years of Reason, she yielded to the desires of the Devil, by ratifying the Engagement she had entred into in her Childhood; but she with another younger Girl were sometimes so touched with Repentance, that she Lamented and Wept when the greatness of her sin and horrible condition were lay'd before her. It was she that Lamented the Death of Madam *B.* for a whole day together, when they resolved to Poyson her upon the first opportunity, with Pills of diabolical Composition, and that discovered the thing to her.

9. Madam *B.* asked her some time after, why instead of continuing of the Cabal that had conspired her Death,she had on the contrary so much lamented it,and discovered the Plot? She answered, *Because I love you more than the Devil, and had rather be faithful to you than to him: Oh that I could but e-*

scape

escape his Snares ! But I cannot : He has too great access to me. I would to God that when you speak to me, and that when I find my Heart touched with Repentance and lament my Misfortune, that somebody was present to cut my Throat ; I should then have hope of Grace and of Salvation ; but otherwise I am lost and cannot be saved : For as soon as you leave me, the Devil returns and does accost me by Caresses, by Threatnings, by Kindnesses ; and never leaves me till seeing me without any Body to help, he regains my consent, and I give my self to him again. Nothing can deliver me from him without taking me out of the World when I am in a state of Repentance, as sometimes I am. To let me live longer, is but to remit me into the power of the Devil. Oh ! how glad would I be if any Body would kill me out of Charity, when I deplore my Misery. These were the complaints of this poor Creature, (a just Object of Pity) made to Madam B. Nevertheless, she did not obtain the favour she desired : For having always held firm in the attestation which she made before the Court, that she was a Witch, instead of putting her to Death, as she desired, she was shut up in Prison, and it was never known what became of her since.

Such Witches so capable of Repentance, are very rare. However, it thereby appears, that the Law of God, which commands not to suffer a Witch to Live, was not only a Law of Justice, but also a Law of Charity ; and that what you call shewing them Mercy, is a great Cruelty, since that Death may conduce to Salvation to those who are capable to Repent, and Life would certainly be pernicious : And for those who are not capable to Repent, it were better that they should go to all the Devils, rather than multiply their Crimes upon Earth, whereby they would augment their eternal Pains.

A

A Relation of a Yarmouth *Witch, who with Fifteen more Convicted upon their own Confessions, was Executed,* 1644.

IN the Year 1644. at *Yarmouth* were sixteen Women accused for Witches by Mr. *Hopkins,* and by the Magistrates sent to Mr. *Whitfeild* and Mr. *Brinsley* Ministers of that Place, to be by them Examined. Among these was an Old Woman who used to be relieved twice a Week at Mr. *Whitfeild's* Door, who made this *Confession*; That she using to work for Mr. *Moulton* (a Stocking Merchant and Alderman of the Town) went to his House for Work, but he being from Home, his Man refused to let her have any till his Master came home, which was not expected in less than a Fortnight's time; whereupon being *Exasperated* against the Man, she applied her self to the Maid, and desired some Knitting Work of her; and when she returned the like Answer, she went home in great discontent and anger against them both: That that Night when she was in Bed, she heard one knock at her Door, and rising to her Window, she saw, it being Moon light, *a tall black Man* there; and asking what he would have? He told her that he understood that she was *Discontented,* because she could not get Work, as she expected; and that he would put her into a way that she should never want either Work or any thing else; whereupon she let him in, and asked him what he had then to say to her? He told her, he must first see her Hand; and then taking out something like a Pen-knife, he gave it *a little Scratch,* so that Blood followed, and the Mark remained to that time, which she then shewed them; then he took some of the Blood in a Pen, and pulling a Book out of his Pocket, bid her *write her Name*; and when she said, she could not, he said, he would guide her Hand, and thereupon did so, and wrote

her

her Name in his Book. When this was done, he bid her now ask what she would have: And when she desired first to be revenged of the Man, he promised to give her an account of it the next Night, and so leaving her some Mony, went away for that time. The next Night he came to her again, and told her he could do nothing against the Man; for he *went constantly to Church* to hear *Whitfeild* and *Brinsly*, and *said his Prayers Morning and Evening*. Then she desired him to revenge her on *the Maid*; and he again promised her to give her an account thereof the next Night; but then he said the same of the Maid, and that therefore he could not hurt her: But he said, that there was a young Child in the House, which was more easie to be dealt with. Whereupon she desired him to do what he could against it: And the next Night he came again, and brought with him an Image of Wax, and told her they must go and Bury that in the Church-yard, and then the Child which he had put into great pain already should waste and consume away as that Image wasted. Whereupon they went together, and he dug a hole with a Spade which he brought with him, and they Buried it. And when he left her, he bid her when ever she wanted any thing, but wish for him to come, and he would presently be with her. The Child having at this time lain in a Languishing condition for about Eighteen Months, and being very near to Death, the Minister sent this Woman with this account to the Magistrates, who thereupon sent her to Mr. *Moulton*'s; where in the same Room where the Child lay almost Dead, she was again Examined concerning the Particulars aforesaid; all which she confessed again, and had no sooner done, but the Child, who was but three Years old, and was thought to be Dead or Dying, Laughed, and began to stir and raise up it self; and from that Instant began to Recover. It was then late in the Night before they had done, so that they could not then search for the Image of Wax, but ordered it to be done early the next Morning; and then the Woman being led to the Church-yard, set her Foot upon a certain place,

and

and faid, that was the place where it was Buried. But tho they dug and fought for it as well as they could, they could find nothing; whether becaufe it was fo wafted, that they loft the relicks of it in the Digging, or removed by the Devil, or whatever elfe was the reafon, it could not be found; but the Child Recovered. This Woman and all the reft were *Convicted* upon their own Confeffions, and were *Condemned, and Executed* accordingly. They had all their *Familiars*, and this Womans did ufually appear in the form of a Black-Bird.

This from a Son of Mr. Whitfeild, *who was then prefent; and to this I fhall fubjoin another of like nature in fome Particulars, which tho I had it but at fecond hand, and therefore probably may not be compleat in all particulars, yet had I it from a competent Relator, who had the firft Relation from an ancient credible Perfon, who was then a Scholar in* Oxford, *when the Tryal was, and I doubt not but related truly what he received concerning the particulars here remembred, as followeth.*

A brief Relation of one faid to be Condemned and Executed at Oxford, in the time of King Charles the Firft.

IN this time, (but the Year is not remembred) a Man Died there, leaving two Daughters, and good Portions to each: The Eldeft fomewhat Prodigal, Married a Husband like her felf, who fpent her Portion, got her with Child, and left her: But the Youngeft being very Serious and Religious, ftaid, two or three Years before fhe Married, and then Married a good honeft fober Farmer, fix or feven Miles off, by whom fhe had a Child, and they lived very happily and comfortably together. This moved great Envy againft her in her Sifter, who was reduced to great Straits. In her Paffion the Devil appeared to her, and fhe made a Contract
with

with him, and became a Witch; and he perfwaded her to kill her Sifters Child, as the greateft defpight fhe could do her. For this purpofe fhe often rofe in the Night out of her Bed, got upon a Bed-ftaff, faid certain words, and thereupon was prefently carried away, and was conveyed into the Room where her Sifter with her Husband and Child lay. This her own Child about Seven years of Age, who lay with her, having often obferved her to do, at laft it would do fo too, and thereupon was prefently carried through the Air into the fame Room, where the Mother and fome others were, who after fome time went all away, and the Child being left behind, fell a Crying; at which the Man and his Wife being awakened, and wondering to hear a Child Cry in their Room, the Man arofe and lighted a Candle, and finding the Child, and underftanding by it how it came thither, the next day they acquainted a Juftice of the Peace with the Matter. Whereupon the Sifter was Apprehended, and Committed, and the next Affizes was Tryed for a Witch: And the Child, who was all the while kept from her, being then produced, told how it came into that Room, and what it had feen and hear'd the Mother fay and do; whereupon, the Mother confeffed all the Matter before related. The Judge then ask'd her if fhe had never been there before in that manner? She faid Yes, an hundred times. Then he asked her, How it came to pafs that fhe did not kill the Child all that while? She anfwered, That fhe always found it fo armed with the Prayers of the Parents, that fhe could never have power to do it. Upon her Confeffion, fhe was Condemned, and Executed.

G   A

A Relation of a Lancashire *Witch*, *Tryed* at Worcester, *in the Year*, 1649.

AT *Droitwich* in the County of *Worcester*, a poor Womans Boy in the Month of *May*, looking for his Mother's Cow, espied some Bushes in a Brake to shake, and supposing the Cow to be Brousing there, went to the Place, where he found no Cow, but an Old Woman, who upon his approach said *Boh*, to him; whereupon he presently lost his speech, and could only make a Noise, but could not speak any thing articulately so as could be understood: In this condition he came home to his Mother, made a great Noise, but no body could understand what ailed him, or what he meant. A while after, he ran out, and at Sir *Edward Barret's* Door, found, about one a Clock amongst other poor People, the same old Woman supping up a Mess of hot Pottage, and ran furiously upon her, and threw her Pottage in her Face, and offered some other Violence to her. Whereupon the Neighbours wondering at the condition of the Boy and his rage against the old Woman, and suspecting that she had done him some hurt, Apprehended her, and thereupon she was committed to the Prison, which they there call the *Checker*. At Night the Boy's Mother Lodged him in a Garret over her own Lodging; and in the Morning hearing a great Bustle over her, ran up, and found the Boy gotten out of his Bed with the Leg of a Form in his hand, striking furiously at something in the Window; but saw nothing there that he should strike at. The Boy presently put on his Cloaths, and ran down into the Street towards the Prison, and as he was going endeavouring to speak, found his Speech restored. When he came to the Prison, he asked for the old Woman, and told the Gaoler how she had served him, and how his Speech came to him again in the way.

The

The Gaoler in the mean time suspecting that she had Be-witched the Boy, would not let her have either Meat or Drink, unless she would first say the Lord's Prayer, and bid God bless the Boy; which at last her Hunger forced her to do; and it appeared to be at the same instant, as near as could be guessed, that the Boy had his Speech restored to him. The Boy asked the Gaoler, why he did not keep her faster, but let her come out and trouble him? The Gaoler answered, he had kept her very safe. The Boy replied, No, he had not; for she came and sat in his Chamber Window, and grinned at him; and that thereupon he took up a Form Leg, and therewith gave her two good bangs upon the Arse as she would have scutled from him, before she could get a-way. Whereupon the Gaoler caused some Women to Search her, who found the Marks of two such Strokes upon her, as the Boy said he had given her. All this was Sworn upon her Tryal, by the Boy, his Mother, the Gaoler, and the Women. Upon Examination she was found to be a *Lancashire* Woman, who upon the Scarcity in those Parts, after the Defeat of Duke *Hamilton*, wandred abroad to get Victuals.

Another Relation of a Teuksbury *Witch*, *Tryed at* Gloucester *about the same time.*

AT *Teuksbury* about the same time a Man, who had a Sow and Pigs, observing his Sow to have great store of Milk, and yet the Pigs to be almost Famished, and con-sulting with his Neighbours about it, they all concluded, that she must needs be Sucked by something else, and so the *Pigs be robbed of the Milk*: Whereupon he resolved to watch till he found out the Matter: And having placed himself conveniently for that purpose, at last he saw a black Four-footed Creature like a Pole-Cat, come and beat away the Pigs, and suck the Sow: And having a Pick, or Fork in his

Hand,

Hand, he ran the Prongs into the Thigh of it, and ran it to the Ground; yet it ftruggled fo as to get off from him at laft. There were fome Neighbours not far off, but they faw no fuch Creature, but faw a Wench go away, and that Blood fell from her as fhe went; whereupon they fearched her, and found her fo Wounded as the Man faid he had wounded the thing which he found Sucking: And thereupon fhe was Apprehended and Tryed at *Gloucefter* Affizes; where this Matter was given in Evidence againft her.

Thefe two Relations I received from a Perfon of Quality, of good Ability, and of unqueftionable Credit, who was prefent at both the Tryals, and wrote them in his prefence; and afterwards read them to him; and he affured me they were very true in all the Particulars, as they were given in Evidence.

A Relation of the grievous Affliction of Faith Corbet, *by the fecret wicked Practices of* Alice Hufon *and* Dol. Bilby, *all of the Parifh of* Burton Agnes *in the County of* York, *from the Year,* 1660, *to the Year,* 1664.

MRs. *Corbet,* Wife of *Henry Corbet,* of *Burton Agnes* in the County of *York,* about the Year 1660, employed one *Alice Hufon* Widow, of the fame Place, about fome fmall matters, as keeping of young Turkies, *&c.* For which, fhe offered to have paid her in Mony, Corn, or otherwife to her Satisfaction; but fhe refufed all, and defired only fome piece of old Linen, which her Children wore next their Skin, to make her a Neckcloth, as fhe pretended. The Children hearing of it, intreated their Mother not to give her any thing that belonged to them, becaufe there went a general evil Report of her in the Town, and many not only accounted her fo, but called her Witch. Mrs. *Corbet* reproved
them

them for faying fo, and to give her content, cut an old
Sheet, made her a Neck-cloth, fent for her, and would have
given it her, but fhe refufed it, defiring only fomething appertaining to the Children, fome piece of old Cloth, which
fome of them wore next their Skin, if it were but as much
as would make a Stay-band; which was denied her; but fhe
frequented the Houfe, and had moft part of her Relief there,
and Mrs. *Corbet* caufed her to be ferved with Meat and
Drink fuch as fhe defired.

One day as *Alice Hufon* was fitting in the Kitchin, her
Daughter *Faith Corbet*, of about Ten or Eleven years of Age,
came in to wafh her Hands, where not fufpecting any thing, fhe
pulled off her Gloves, and wafhing her Hands, when fhe
had done, went into the Houfe to dry them, and then returned prefently again, but her Gloves were gone, and *Alice
Hufon* alfo. Whereupon, fhe often complained for the lofs
of her Gloves, and faid that the Old Witch hod gotten
them, but durft not fpeak it openly, for fear her Mother
fhould chide her: And not long after, fhe fell into *a ftrange
Fit*, fo that two or three could hardly hold her, did often
Screech and Cry out vehemently, fometimes fcratch and bite
any fhe could lay hold on, and fay, Ah, *Alice*, Old Witch,
have I gotten thee? And fometimes lye down all drawn together, almoft round; and lye ftill as in a Swoon, continuing thus the moft part of a Week: And fometimes again all
of a fudden, fhe became unufually Merry, and continued fo
for a confiderable time together.

In thefe Fits, many came to vifit her, and various were
their Opinions of them; fome faying they were Fits of the
Mother; others, that they proceeded from the Mother and
the Spleen; others, that they were Convulfion Fits, *&c.* And
divers Phificians were Confulted for her. For, her Father
obferving daily and almoft hourly the motions and alterati-
ons of her Diftemper, wrote to Dr. *Taylor*, (who lived at
York) and defcribed the fame to him as exactly as he could.
The Doctor was very confident he could grapple with any
Difeafe Curable, except there was Fafcination in the cafe:

But

But in this his Skill failed; and therefore, when several things which he thought good for her, had been used, but did her no good, her Father sent to Dr. *Whitty*, who being then at *Beverly*, came over to her, staid that Night and the next Day till after Noon, greatly admiring the manner of her Fits, and gave her sometimes one thing, and sometimes another, as he thought convenient for her; but she was little the better. Her Distemper still continuing, or rather returning at times (for she had intervals) her Father upon the 24*th*. of *March*, 1660, carried her to *Hull* to Dr. *Corbet*, who with his Wife, (who it seems had some skill in such Distempers) used their utmost Endeavours, but with little Success. Whereupon she was fetched home; and after some time continuing ill, she desired to go to her Sisters at *Dalby Daile* in *Pickering Lath*, hoping that the change of the Air and a remote Place, might conduce to her Health, or Recovery; but about 15 *February*, 1661, she fell extream ill, so that her Father was sent for, and forced to go to *York* for Advice, tho much against her mind; for she said, *Doctors nor Physick could do her no good*, still crying out against *Alice Huson*; and the 9*th* of *March* he brought her home again. Where her Fits and Distemper still continuing, and growing more violent, Doctor *Taylor* having been several times with her, desired her Father to send her to *York*, where he would have an eye and 'special care over her. So the 18*th* of ——— 1662, he carried her thither, where she remained till the 21 of *May*, 1663. But she still continuing ill, entreated her Father to let her take no more *Physick*; for nothing would cure her so long as those too, *Alice Huson* and *Dol. Bilby*, were at Liberty, frequently crying out of them. And her Fits at times still growing more violent, she desired once more to see her Sister at *Dolby*, and the rather because her Sister being with Child, was near her time of Travel. Whereupon she was sent thither 4*th*. *March*, 1663. And the 22*d*. as she was lying in Bed with her Sister, her Sister that Night fell in Travel, and desired her to rise and call her Mother; which she going to do, as she was going out of the Chamber door, a *Black Cat*, as

she

she said, leaped in her Face, (tho there was no such known to be in the House) and so affrighted her, that she got into her Sisters Bed, and clasped such fast hold on her, then in Travel of Child-birth, that the Women who came in to her Labour, could scarce get her from her : She still crying out of *Bilby* and *Huson*, continuing there with her Sister, some times well, and sometimes ill. Her Father was sent for again 3*d.* of *April,* 1664. Who finding her in a very sad condition, unknown to her, sent again to Doctor *Taylor* to *York*, and received Cordials and other Physick from him ; which when she understood, she told him, ' That if she had ' known, he should not have sent, for all the Doctors and ' Physick in the World could do her no good, so long as ' those two Women were at Liberty ; they would have her ' Life, and she was contented, since she could not be believ- ' ed. There she continued most violently handled, so that her Father was constrained to borrow Sir *Fr. Boynton*'s Coach to carry her home, 9. *April,* expecting daily and hourly when she should depart and give up her Life ; but especially the 22*d.* of *April* her Fits seized her in a most strange and violent manner, for Twenty two Hours together, without the least intermission ; so that every one thatsaw her, thought it impossible she should live one Minute. Her Tongue hung out at a large extent ; her Teeth so hard set fast, that it was feared she would bite off her Tongue ; she lay as Dead, with her Eyes broad open ; Her Arms and Legs and Thighs twisted and admirably twined together ; her Bowels by the report of Women that came in to see her and sat up with her, so drawn up together, that one might have laid their Hand upon her Belly and have felt her Back-bone, and her Spleen taken quite away, but she had the benefit of Hearing and Understanding ; so that being asked by those that were about her, who troubled her ? She could answer sometimes *Bilby*, sometimes *Huson*, and sometimes both together. She remaining in this condition, Sir *Francis Boynton* advised her Father to send for the Doctors ; he sent to *York* and *Hull* for Dr. *Taylor*, Dr. *Whitty* and Dr. *Corbet* : But e'er they came, she coming

a

a little to her felf began thus to fpeak, *Oh Faithlefs and incredulous People! Shall I never be believed till it be paft time? For I am as near Death as poffibly may be; and when they have got my Life, you will repent when it is paft time.* Hereupon her Father went to Mr. *Wellfet*, Minifter of *Burton Agnes,* and they and others went to fpeak with *Alice Hufon*, and tho at firft they could not prevail with her yet at laft they got her to his Houfe, and Sir *Fr. Boynton* a Juftice of the Peace and Mr. *Wellfet* being there, after much a do, at laft they prevailed with her to go up into his Daughters Chamber. As fhe went up, his Daughter gave a great Screech; and fome in the Chamber brought *Alice Hufon* to the Bed-fide: And after a fhort time, fhe going down again, his Daughter called fuddenly for a Toaft and Beer; for (fhe faid) fhe was very Hungry and Dry. All were amazed to fee fo fudden a Change, for fhe had not taken any thing in three days before, and was fo weak, that fhe defired always thofe who were with her, to turn her in her Bed. Having taken her Toaft and Beer, fhe faid, if they would give her fome of her Cordials, fhe could take them, which before fhe could not; and having taken a good quantity, fhe defired, to the admiration of all who faw her before, to have her Cloaths, and fhe got up and told them how fhe had been handled by the two Women. She continued well all *Saturday* Night, and *Sunday* Morning 24th. of *April,* all the Doctors met and confulted about her Cafe; and coming to her fpake comfortably to her, and told her how they had confulted for her good. She anfwered, and faid, *I thank you Gentlemen, for your Pains, Care and good Will: But if my Father would have been perfwaded by me, he fhould not have fent for you: For I know, that fo long as thofe two women are at Liberty, neither you nor any other, or any thing you can adminifter, will do me any good: But I muft to give my Father and you fatisfaction, take fuch as you give me.* Thus fhe continued in a good State (faith her Father) till after Dinner I went up, and ftaid till Church time, and then left her as I fuppofed in a good condition. When I came to the Door, to go to Church, *Doll. Bilby* (who as we fuppofed had

had been with *Alice Huson*) came by, whereupon I ftaid ftill, and let her pafs by, obferving her Gefture; and when fhe came againft the Window of the Chamber where my Daughter lay, fhe turned about, and looked up at the Window ; and immediately my Daughter cried out, fhe is there ; and giving a great Screek, fell again into her *Fits*, crying out, her Heart was quite gone. On *Monday* 25 of *April*, *Bilby* came again to Town, (She lived at *Thorne Hotime*, which is in the fame Parifh of *Burton Agnes*) and had Conference with *Huson*, as *Huson* confeffed. But my Daughter fell fo ill again, continually blaming them, and faying they had too much Liberty, that that Night I got them Secured, the 26th. Examined, the 27th, Searched, the 28th, Re-examined, and *Alice Huson* Confeffed; and the 29th, *Bilby* Examined again, upon *Huson*'s Confeffion, and both fent to the Gaol. But this is to be obferved, that tho my Daughter was well (juft) before, yet upon their Examination and Searching, and during all that time, fhe was moft cruelly handled and tormented, and as foon as they were Carted, fhe Recovered, (and) continued fo till *Saturday* 14th. of *May*, when fhe fell fuddenly into her old Fits, affirming that *Bilby* had got Pins and Needles, wherewith fhe Tormented her, and had too much Liberty. On *Monday* Morning I went to *York*, and found it was as fhe faid, and Mr. *Read* the Keeper, faid, fhe fhould be foon held and reftrained of her Liberty ; and faid, obferve the time of the Day; it is upon the point of Two; and faid as foon as you are out of the Caftle-Gate, all fhall be done, therefore let me hear how your Daughter doth. Coming home, I found my Daughter (bleffed be God) in good Health. I enquired what time fhe Recovered? they faid, upon the point of Two fhe called for her Cloaths, and faid fhe would Rife, for fhe was fure her Father had been at the Caftle, and gotten her Bufinefs done.

All this is taken from a Paper written by the before-mentioned Henry Corbet *himself* : *And here followeth*,

H   *The*

The Confeſſion of Alice Huſon, 28 *of* April, 1664. *to Mr.* Tim. Wellfet, *Vicar of* Burton Agnes, (*in her own Words*) *as it was given in to the Judges at* York *Aſſizes,*

THree Years I have had to do with, and for the Devil: He appeared to me like a *Black Man* on a Horſe upon the Moor: He told me I ſhould never want, if I would follow his ways: He bid me to give my ſelf to him, and forſake the Lord; and I promiſed him I would. He did upon that give me five Shillings; and another time he gave me ſeven Shillings: And for ſix ſeveral times he did ſo; and *Thom. Ratle* had 20 *s*. of the Mony I had of him. He appeared like a *Black Man* upon a Black Horſe, with Cloven-Feet; and then I fell down, and did Worſhip him upon my Knees, becauſe I promiſed him I would do ſo. I have hurt Mrs. *Faith Corbet* by my Evil Spirit: I did, in my apprehenſion, ride her: And when I was Examined by Mr. *Wellfet* our Miniſter, the Devil ſtood by, and gave me my Anſwer. I was under the Window like a Cat, when Mrs. *Corbet* ſaid I was; and *Doll Bilby* had a hand in this Tormenting Mrs. *Corbet*: *Doll Bilby* ſaid, let us make an End of her ; and I ſaid it was pity to take away her Life, for we had done her overmuch hurt already. The Devil did appear to me and *Doll Bilby* both together: *Doll Bilby* had of the Devil on *Thurſday* or *Friday*, ſome Mony : I had about a Fortnight ago ten Shillings of the Devil at *Ratle*'s door about Twi-light or Day-gate; and I gave two Shillings of this Mony for two Pecks of Barly, Peaſe and Wheat mix'd, to *Will. Parkley*: He told me, if I would kill Mrs. *Alice Corbet*, I ſhould never Want : He twitches me at the Heart, as if it were drawn together with Pincers. I have, I confeſs, a Witch-pap, which is Sucked by the Unclean Spirit: This Sucking laſteth from

Supper-

Supper-time, till after Cock-crowing. The Devil did bid me deny to Mr. *Wellfet* that he was sent by me. I had a purpose to practice Witchcraft when I begg'd a piece of Cloth and Black-hood. I confess that I did by this Evil Spirit, kill *Dick Warren*; which was done by my wicked Heart and wicked Eyes: If I had not employ'd this wicked Spirit, I had not hurt him. I lent *Lancelot Harrison* eight Shillings of the ten Shillings the Devil gave me. I did forsake God, because I promised the Devil to serve him. The Devil bid me not to tell of *Doll Bilby.*

This is the full Confession of Alice Huson *in her own words, suited to the Questions I propounded to her, being spoken to my self; (so) I testifie.*

Timothy Wellfet,
Vicar of Burton
Agnes.

A horrible Relation of a Trumpeter, *his Wife and Daughter, Debauched by a Wicked foul Spirit. Transcribed from a Letter, written by a very Intelligent Person in* Holland.

A *Trumpeter,* who had served the Prince in his Wars, upon his return from the War, finding many Executed for Witchcraft in that Country, absented himself, and hid himself. He being miss'd, and they knowing no reason for his Absconding, enquiry was made after him, supposing he might hav been guilty of some evil Action or other, Theft, or Adultery, &c. But found nothing against him. However, they continued their Enquiry, till at last they found where he was, and told him he must go to the Prince. Whereupon he cried out, I am a Dead Man. And being

Neither the Country, nor the Time is mentioned in the Letter.

H 2

asked

asked, what was the matter? He said he was a Witch, and must Die. To the Prince he was brought; before whom (to the amazement of him and all Men, for none suspected him in the least) he confessed, that one day walking in the Wood, he had met in a By Walk, a very handsom Woman, with whom entring into Discourse, he endeavoured to perswade her to submit to his Will, which at last she yielded to; and when he had satisfied himself with her, she Transformed her self into a hideous Shape, and told him, Now he was from that time forward his; but made him many Promises, &c. He being thus Engaged, said he had a Wife, and wished her in the same Condition. This Caco-Dæmon replied, he should take no care for that matter; he would effect it, and thus; He should pretend a necessity of going from Home all of a sudden, and tell his Wife that there would come to find him a Gentleman, a good Friend of his in the War; and that he was sorry he could not stay to receive him as he would, desiring her, if he came before he returned, to make as much of him as she could possible, as being his singular Friend. He being gone, this pretended Gentleman some time after, came in very good Equipage, attended with a Servant, enquired for her Husband, seemed sorry for his Absence: But she doing her Errand as her Husband had ordered her, and shewing him great Kindness, he propounded to her the having his Will upon her; and she consenting, he enjoyed her not only, but her Daughter (also) of about Eleven, or twelve Years Old, to whom then he appeared as to her Husband: And then her Husband returned and found it so.

From that time forward, certain power to hurt Cattle (as I remember) only was imparted to them: And the Man was continually accosted and compelled to continue his Commerce with his *Succuba*, and the Woman and her Daughter with their *Incubus*; with whom the first Commerce was strangely Delightful, but ever after cold and painful to them.

Thefe

Thefe things having Confefs'd, and being very penitent, they defired to die, and were accordingly Executed: But becaufe they had not hurt Mankind, and were fo Penitent, inftead of being Burn'd, they were Beheaded.

The Prince would fain have faved the Girl, becaufe of her Youth, and ufed all Endeavours to deliver her from the Spirit, but could not effect it; the Girl crying out feveral times that he now was committing Uncleannefs with her; crying out and defiring rather to die than to live fo, and be fubject to that foul Spirit any longer, and accordingly was Executed as her Father and Mother were.

A Relation of a Dutch *Boy*, Poffeffed *by a* German *Spirit. Being an Extract of two Letters, the firft, of the* 12 *of* Febbruary, 1690. S. V.

WE have here a ftrange Cafe of a Youth about Fifteen Years old, that has been of a quiet and orderly Converfation, and was bred up to Reading and Praying, who is Poffeffed, and as the Spirit it felf fays through him, is actuated by three of them, who were fent to him by three divers Witches, which he publickly named.

I my felf have entred the Lifts with the Ghoft, who at laft, tho very unwillingly, Anfwered, and fpeaks as good High *Dutch* as is fpoken in *Auftria*, which the Lad could never fpeak. I was very fharp in my Affault, and he as ftrenuoufly oppofed. When he departs, it is with a great Noife, and the Lad lyes a good while as in a deep Swoon, till recovered by application of fit Remedies, and then he prays devoutly, which while Poffeffed, he cannot do; and when the Spirits forfake him in part, which fometimes they do for a whole, fometimes for half a day; he works at his ordinary Labour, which is, Weaving Linen, that being the Trade he is Learning. He is of a Meek Spirit; but in his Fits, three Men have enough to hold him.

The

The Spirit says very confidently, that he has leave from the Old Man in Heaven (Thus he calls *God*, and will not easily be brought to use that word) not to leave the Lad till the Witches have received their Punishments; and that he was compelled by that Old Man in Heaven to discover the Witches and their wicked Works; all which he has done, and upon it, the Inquest was made, which otherwise no body would have thought of.

In fine, it is so strange and incomprehensible a thing, that 'tis not to be expressed, insomuch, that if I had not been an eye Witness, and throughly examined the Affair, I could never have believed it.

The Second Letter of the 24th. *of* April, S. V. 1690.

NOw again something of the Possessed Lad: Our Discourse went upon these five things. 1. Of the great Omnipotency of the true God, and his sole Government over all things, both Visible and Invisible. 2. Of the glorious Merits of Christ his Sufferings, and thereby overturning of the Powers of Hell: And consequently. 3. Of the Limited, and in it self powerless Power of the Devils, &c. Of their Orders and Qualities among themselves. 4. Of the great Power of the Holy Ghost, dwelling in a true Believer and Pious Soul. 5. Of the Name of this particular Spirit, that speaks out of the Possessed Lad, his Authority, and the cause of his cruel Works.

As to the First, he answered all my Questions affirmatively, and confessed, that all things, even their Infernal Government, are executed according to the Will *of God*: But that word he would not name, till he was constrained by a Command in the Name of the most High, which then he uttered storming. Then I proceeded to all the Ordinary Attributes of God, which tho against his will, he owned, saying with a roaring Voice, Yes, it is true.

At

At the Second, he grew very impatient, Gnaſhing with his Teeth, and would not name the name of *Chriſt*, till I conſtrained him as before, and alledged the Example of the Devil in the Goſpel, that had ſpoke concerning Chriſt.

I Then proceeded to the Third, Whereupon he acknowledged an Order amongſt them, but would not confeſs of what Order himſelf was, but ſaid, *Thou askeſt more than is needful for thee to know.*

I replied, *But thou knoweſt well enough, that I know full well what pitiful things you Spirits are without God's Permiſſion.*

He. *I know it, or elſe thou would'ſt forbear to vex me thus.*

I. *How comeſt thou to be ſuch a ſilly Devil, that thou canſt ſpeak nothing but High Dutch?*

He. *Are you Men then all of the ſame Capacity?*

I paſſed then to the former things, and ſpake to him of the *Blood of Chriſt*, &c.

He. *I'll be gone.*

I. *No, thou ſhalt firſt anſwer me to this.*

He anſwered, *I know Chriſt has redeemed Men, and therefore we can do nothing to you without Permiſſion*: And repeated divers times, *I'll be gone.*

At laſt I ſaid, *Go then and be Hanged.* And immediately he went forth with a great Outcry; whereupon the poor Lad being come as out of an Extaſie, after divers applications, returned to himſelf again.

I asked the Devils *their Names*; he ſaid his Name was *Pretty Betty*; the other was call'd *Longtale*, and the third, *Cuckow*: and theſe three poſſeſſed the Lad, whereof two go forth, but one of them keeps always poſſeſſion of the Body.

The

The next day, being the day of the Circumcifion of *Chrift*, I went on where I left off the day before, and fo came,

To the Fourth, Of the Holy Ghoft, which he refifted hard, but at laft owned all that I demanded on that head; but within half an hour would be gone: But I would not let him go according to his will, till he had anfwered me fully; and then he went away, as the day before.

If we interrogate the Devil too profoundly, or too curioufly, he anfwers, *Thou askeft more than is fit for thee to know, or permitted to me to fay.*

Three German Miles from hence, dwells one Mr. *Crom*, whofe little Daughter of about Twelve Years Old, is in like manner poffeffed; out of whom the Devil fpeaks all manner of Languages imaginable.

The E N D.